Molly

MOMMY?

Other books by Tamra Norton:

MOLLY MORMON?

MOLLY MARRIED?

COMFORTABLE IN MY OWN GENES

Also available on Audio CD

Molly
MOMMY?

TAMRA NORTON

Bonneville Books
Springville, Utah

ISBN: 1-55517-831-6
v.1

Published by Bonneville Books,
an imprint of Cedar Fort, Inc.
925 N. Main Springville, Utah, 84663
www.cedarfort.com

Distributed by:

Cover design by Nicole Williams
Cover design © 2005 by Lyle Mortimer

Printed in the United States of America
10 9 8 7 6 5 4 3 2 1

Printed on acid-free paper

Dedication

To *my* mommy, Lynne Poulton; and my mommy-in-law, Edna Norton—two incredible ladies! And to all of you who have grown to love Molly and asked for more.

Acknowledgments

I'd like to thank the wonderful folks at Cedar Fort for their encouragement and support in helping bring Molly, a spirited, lovable, and unforgettable character, into the lives of so many readers who have come to love her as much as I do.

I owe a great debt of appreciation to Marie Gossling and her daughters Grace and Julie for reading the first draft of every chapter as it was "born" and for giving me such insightful and honest feedback.

Thanks to the LDStorymakers—a group of incredibly talented authors and some of my dearest friends. You continue to make me smile and laugh every day. Thanks for challenging me to become a better writer as well.

And a big thank-you to my wonderful family for embracing my creative side—even if it means eating frozen pizza and corn dogs on a regular basis. I love you very much!

Chapter
ONE

"Molly, this is for you." Mrs. Schultz, my boss and the manager of the Idaho State University Bookstore, handed me a white envelope during a rare slow moment at the cash register. Then she turned around and walked back into her office. The fall semester had started two weeks earlier, and traffic in the bookstore was finally settling down to a manageable flow.

Kassie, my coworker and salvation during those hectic afternoon hours, leaned over from her register next to mine in an attempt to get my attention. "What was *that* all about?"

I shrugged my shoulders as I turned the long white envelope over and over in my hands. A sense of dread began to settle deep within my stomach. Was I being reprimanded, or worse, fired? That would be awful. As newlyweds and full-time students, Gordon and I were barely surviving on ramen noodles and macaroni and cheese. Okay, I'm exaggerating—a little. We also ate a lot of peanut butter and jelly sandwiches and homemade potato soup. How could we possibly make ends meet if I lost this job?

"Are you going to open it or just stare at it?" Kassie asked.

"Okay, okay," I replied as I slid my finger under the corner flap of the envelope and began to rip the seal.

As I pulled out a folded piece of pink construction paper, my stomach quickly settled, and my heart began to swell. I immediately noticed that familiar handwriting on the outside of an obviously homemade card.

"Sooooo, what is it?" Since there weren't any customers at the moment, Kassie had walked around her register and was now standing at my side.

I showed her the front of the card, and she read it out loud. "Happy

Anniversary." My friend and coworker's voice suddenly elevated in pitch. "Oooooh, how sweet! I had no idea it was your anniversary today."

I couldn't help but smile. "It's not."

"Then why the anniversary card?" I could hear the confusion in Kassie's voice but could only offer one explanation.

"That's just Gordon." I opened the card and read the words to myself.

To my Molly on our "Triple-3" anniversary. The past three months, three weeks, and three days have been the best of my life. I swapped schedules with Todd so we could celebrate tonight. I'll pick you up as soon as you get off work.

I love you, Molly.

Yours, Gordon

"Well?" Kassie asked.

"He loves me," I replied and began to read the contents of the card for a second time.

"And . . . ?" Over the past two months of working with Kassie, I had learned that the girl was a hopeless romantic. And impatient. She was obviously fishing for details, so I decided to put her out of her misery and handed her the card.

Mrs. Schultz walked out of her office again, so Kassie, with card in hand, wandered back to her register and tried to look busy. I could tell, however, that she was dying to read the card.

Classes must have let out because the bookstore suddenly became busy. A line soon formed at my register, and for the next twenty-five minutes I hardly had time to think of anything beyond scanning textbooks, school supplies, and other student paraphernalia. These moments were both welcomed and dreaded. Staying busy like this definitely made time pass by quickly, but it was also monotonous work—you've scanned one textbook, you've scanned a million. It certainly helped to keep my educational goals in perspective; I didn't want to be standing at a register for the rest of my life.

Finally, with fifteen minutes left until closing and an almost empty store, Kassie and I wandered over to the magazine and candy racks to straighten things up and, of course, talk.

Kassie withdrew the card from her apron pocket and handed it back to me with a sigh. "I would love to find a guy like Gordon to write me love letters and sweep me off my feet."

A Snickers bar was sitting in the Milky Way box, so I returned it to its proper place while responding, "What about that guy you went out with last week? What was his name?"

"You mean Bruce?" Kassie rolled her eyes as she said his name. "I highly doubt I'll be seeing much of him again outside of our psychology class."

"Why? He seemed pretty nice when he came by to pick you up. Not so bad looking either."

Kassie put her hands on her hips while shifting her weight. "Where should I start? When he put his wad of chewed-up gum on the edge of his dinner plate and then plopped it back in his mouth after eating a barbecue beef sandwich? Or how about when I caught him picking his nose and then wiping it on the floor of his car—disgusting!"

"Everyone picks their nose, Kassie. I'm pretty sure even Gordon does."

I laughed.

Kassie didn't.

We headed over to the office supplies and started straightening the pens and markers. "I want somebody romantic," Kassie continued. "Somebody who will switch his work schedule so that we can celebrate our 'Triple-3' anniversary."

I looked over at Kassie and couldn't help but be reminded of myself only a year earlier when I was attending BYU–Idaho in Rexburg. I was so caught up in the notion of what I thought it would be like to fall in love, so caught up in who I thought the man of my dreams was (and I was wrong, by the way), that I almost didn't recognize him when he literally waltzed into my life in our ballroom dance class. Gordon has been one big surprise after another since we first met.

"The best advice I can give you," I said, "is to expect the unexpected when it comes to falling in love."

"That sounds like a cheesy trailer for a chick flick."

I shrugged my shoulders because I certainly didn't have the answers. The only thing I knew for certain was that I loved Gordon, and he loved me. The rest of our life together would have to find a way of working itself out.

❊❊❊

At 6 P.M. Kassie and I and the other employees left the ISU Bookstore while Mrs. Schultz locked up. I was thrilled that my shift was over and beyond thrilled that I wasn't scheduled to work again until Monday. My homework was already starting to pile up, and I definitely needed the weekend to get a handle on things.

True to his word, Gordon was there to pick me up, and in his hand he held a wrapped box with a little bow on top.

"You got me a gift," I said as Gordon handed over the box. It was then that I noticed the wrapping paper was actually the comic strip section from the Sunday newspaper that our landlords, the Kendalls, gave to us every Monday.

We lived in half of the Kendalls' basement, which had been transformed into an apartment. They had six children, and the apartment gave them an extra income while allowing Sister Kendall to be a stay-at-home mom. And for us, the apartment—which we lovingly referred to as The Cave (the lighting wasn't so great), was simply our little piece of heaven. It had a living room (half of which doubled as a dining area), a hallway-like kitchen, a bathroom, a bedroom, and a very large walk-in closet off of the living room, which we transformed into an office.

"Hey, special days call for special gifts," Gordon said while giving me that impish grin. Even though we'd been married an entire summer, Gordon could still make my heart flutter. Possibly because now that we were man and wife, I hardly ever saw the guy—especially since school started.

Between our respective class schedules and my job at the bookstore and Gordon's jobs tutoring and stocking shelves at Albertsons, sometimes we were together only when we were asleep. To aid in our attempt to stay connected, we kept a journal of sorts—a fifty-cent spiral notebook—on the kitchen table so we could at least communicate in some form. This evening, however, all of our communication would be in person. What a treat!

After giving Gordon a huge hug and kiss, I held up the gift. "Can I open it now?"

"Of course."

Never being one with much patience, I ripped off the wrapping paper to unveil a beautiful box of fudge-covered Oreos—my favorite cookie in the universe. I could hardly control my enthusiasm and gave my husband another enormous hug and kiss outside the bookstore, this time a little longer on the kiss part. Thank goodness my boss and fellow employees had left and the hall was relatively empty.

"I have two more surprises." Gordon said with enthusiasm. "The last one involves a candlelit dinner featuring my spectacular home-made tuna casserole with crumbled-up potato chips on top."

"Mmmmmm." I patted my belly, although I was skeptical about the crumbled potato chip part.

"And the second one is at the gym. We'll have to drive over so I can show it to you."

"You sure are going all out for some hugs and kisses tonight," I said with a smile.

"Actually, I was shooting for the dutiful-and-attentive-husband angle. But now that you mention it . . ." Gordon raised his eyebrows twice, and I couldn't help but laugh.

"You'll get more kisses soon enough," I replied. "Let's go see what this gym business is about. You have my curiosity piqued."

Gordon's rusty old Suburban was parked outside, and in no time we had pulled in front of the Reed Gym, with its huge mascot, an orange and black Bengal tiger statue, standing guard outside.

As we held hands and walked to the entrance, I speculated on this surprise—an almost frightening experience. With Gordon Nelson involved, anything was possible. "Let's see, you reserved the dance studio and we're going to relive our 'Fred and Ginger' days?" Last year at BYU-Idaho we were ballroom dance partners—a fate I will be eternally grateful for.

"Nope. A nice thought, but when did we ever need a dance studio to do a little tango?" Gordon spun me around in the parking lot so I was facing him, but we only got a few steps into our spontaneous little dance before a car started to back out, heading right toward us. Gordon quickly pulled me out of harm's way, and we decided to save the dance for a little later on.

We were only a few feet into the gym when Gordon led me toward a bulletin board and pointed to a notice.

"What do you think?" he prodded.

It took a while for me to say anything because I had to read and then reread the paper. Then I had to digest its contents.

"You really think I should do this?" I asked.

"Why not?" Gordon replied with confidence. "You were the star of your high school basketball team, and you've beat me at every game of one-on-one that we've ever played. You can even beat me at Horse."

"No offense, sweetie. But . . . well . . . you're not exactly Michael Jordan, and neither am I. There's no way I'd make the cut on the ISU women's basketball team."

Gordon tapped the paper. "Look! It says right here that there are two walk-on positions available. I don't see why one of them couldn't be you. You're a natural athlete, Molly. Go for it."

"And when will I fit all the practices into my schedule?"

"You can quit the bookstore. I'll get another part-time job."

"You'd do that for me?"

"I'd do anything to make my Molly happy," Gordon replied, but this time the smile was gone. I knew he was serious.

After giving Gordon yet another kiss, I started leading him back toward the door. "We'll think about it, okay? Now let's go have some tuna casserole. And did you mention something about candlelight?"

Gordon's blue eyes lit up. And once again, my heart fluttered.

Chapter
TWO

As married students enrolled at Idaho State University, Gordon and I decided to attend a married student ward instead of a standard family ward. We figured that in our current newlywed state of being, we'd fit in better amongst the hand-holding, smooch-sneaking, knowledge-seeking, poverty-stricken cave dwellers (remember, we lived in a basement apartment). But, as each Sunday passed, I wondered if maybe we'd made a huge mistake.

Bulging bellies and bawling babies seemed to abound in our new worshiping environment, which, I guess, should be no huge surprise. But, when you happen to be the only person within spit-up range in the entire Relief Society who's not in "the family way"—or at least, it looks that way—you start to feel a little left out. Every conversation seemed to revolve around breastfeeding, the frequency of baby bowel-movements, or something called Braxton-Hicks—which I prayed wasn't contagious.

It's not that I didn't want to have babies. Actually, I did. And Gordon did too. But apparently Heavenly Father wasn't ready for us to take this step yet. And to be honest, at times I had doubts that I was even cut out for motherhood. How could I know for sure that I'd even wake up in the middle of the night to my baby's cries? For six straight years of girl's camp I was a favorite recipient of middle-of-the-night pranks and gags because of my deep-sleeping tendencies. And then there's the whole diaper-changing issue, which I'd just rather not think about due to my keen sense of smell and easily triggered gag reflex.

Heaven help me—and my future children!

So when Sunday afternoon, and the close of our meetings, arrived, I must admit that I was relieved to be back at The Cave where

I no longer had to deal with that ever-present aroma of Desitin. (At first I was impressed that all these new-mommies had what appeared to be French manicures—until I realized the white under their finger tips was just the remains of diaper rash ointment).

Gordon and I had just sat down, ready to enjoy a wonderful, warmed-up plate of leftover tuna casserole, when a knock sounded at the door. I was about to stand up, but Gordon motioned me to stay seated.

"I'll get it. You start eating," he said as he stood up and ascended the flight of stairs leading to our front door (which was almost hidden on the side of the Kendall's house).

It didn't take long for me to figure out who it was. I could recognize my younger brother's distinct voice from any typical crowd of sports fans.

"Hey, Curt. Come on down," I hollered. "We're having tuna casserole." Funny how he had a keen ability of showing up whenever food was being served.

"Did you make it, Molly?" My brother asked as he came into view. "Because if you did, well, maybe I'll just make myself a PB&J."

I not-so-playfully slugged my little brother in the arm. "My cooking's not *that* bad."

Gordon intervened, "You're safe, Bro. I made the masterpiece, although it looked a lot better last night."

"It still tastes good." I spoke with my mouth full. Nobody seemed to mind. Gordon handed Curt his already-full plate, motioned to an empty chair, and then went into the kitchen to retrieve another plate.

You'd have thought the kid was half-starved the way he consumed Gordon's tuna casserole. Then again, he was still a growing teenager—eighteen, to be exact. After graduating from Oakley High School, my not-so-little brother (the kid had muscles on top of muscles) decided to attend Idaho State University until he turned nineteen in May and was eligible to serve a two-year mission for the Church.

Curt held up his fork, "Gordon, this stuff beats a PB&J any day, and, trust me, I'm becoming quite an expert at making it."

Gordon nodded in thanks.

I turned to face my brother. "So how's life over at the bachelor pad?" He had moved into an apartment with Paul Bloom from Oakley and a few other guys he'd never met until the day he moved in.

Curt rolled his eyes and let out a big sigh before speaking. "I like to have fun as much as the next guy—at least I thought I did—but it's just plain craziness over there. No one sleeps—at least not until two or three in the morning—and I have a seven o'clock class on Monday, Wednesday, and Friday. Some of my groceries have come up missing. And when I want to study, someone always has their stereo blasting—if not one of my roommates then one of the guys next door."

A sympathetic smile played across Gordon's face. "I sure don't miss those bachelor pad days. I feel for ya, Dude. I wish I could help."

"Well, actually, maybe you can." Curt had a hopeful expression. This worried me.

"What do you mean?" Gordon asked before heaping a spoonful of tuna and noodles into his mouth.

Curt took a deep breath before speaking. "One of my roommates has a friend who wants to move into the apartment. The guy's family lives here in Pocatello, but he thinks he's missing out on all the fun by living at home. I told him he could buy my contract if I could find another place to live. Someplace a little more quiet. Like here, with you two."

You could almost hear my now-full stomach trying to digest my food as Gordon and I looked at each other, trying to digest this thought. Just what every newlywed couple dreams of: sharing their first apartment with the bride's kid brother. How romantic. Please, someone pass the Lysol; I can already smell the stinky sport socks. Was my little brother crazy? Obviously he thought we were.

"Now there's a thought," Gordon said, and I could see the cogs turning in his brain. This definitely wasn't good, and I began to wonder if my eternal companion was actually delusional. Was he seriously, for one minute, considering this as a possibility?

"Yeah," I replied. "And here's another thought, sweetie." I usually didn't call Gordon names like "sweetie" and "honey," but I felt it was necessary ammunition to help deliver the startling fact to the two non-rational, commonsense-deprived males sitting before me. "Um, Gordon, did you forget that we're *newlyweds?*"

Gordon's eyes got big—a dangerous sign. "Actually, this just might be a perfect situation all around."

"Yeah, all around the doghouse, which is where both of you will be sleeping if you don't quit talking crazy!"

Curt looked at me with dejection seeping from every pore before finally speaking. "Molly's right, Gordon. It would be wrong for me to interfere in your lives at this point." My little brother looked about as sincere as a turnip.

"But actually, the timing couldn't be more perfect. We could set up a bedroom in our office for you." Gordon stood up and pointed to the huge walk-in closet. He was downright serious. "And with the money you can pitch in, Molly can quit her job at the bookstore and try out for the basketball team. Yes, it's perfect!"

Perfect? Did my husband just say perfect? Snow on Christmas Eve—now that's perfect. Watching a chick flick with your best girlfriend while sharing a bag of popcorn, a tall lemonade, and a box of Raisinettes—now that's perfect. Being completely pimple-free and a size five on the day of your wedding—well, you just can't get more perfect than that. But letting your little brother, who for half of your life referred to you as *Molly Moo-Cow*, move in with you (especially while you're a newlywed) is nothing short of lunacy and I wasn't going to have anything to do with it. Maybe *I'd* have to move out to the dog house.

"Molly?" My husband of three months, three weeks and four days was looking at me with those irresistibly clear blue eyes that could easily coerce me into doing things that my rational self would never consider—like eating frog legs or letting my little brother move into The Cave with us so that I could quit my job and try out for the ISU Women's Basketball team.

I turned to Curt, whose look of desperation was almost convincing. "You've seen our office, right? It's nothing more than a huge closet. There isn't even a window."

Now Curt was smiling. "I like it pitch black when I sleep."

"You can probably stand in the middle and touch both walls," I continued.

Now Gordon stepped in. "There's room for a twin-size bed in there. And probably even a dresser and a small nightstand."

"And where will we put the computer?" I countered.

"In our bedroom. Besides, you only use it in the evenings when I'm working, right?"

The way things were going, I could probably conjure up a hundred logical reasons why this wasn't a good idea. And these two guys, whom I happened to not only love deeply but also trust emphatically—even with my life—would just counter my logic with convincing arguments supporting their stance.

I let out a deep sigh, threw my hands in the air, and looked into the anxious eyes of my little brother. "Okay, okay. Welcome to The Cave."

Curt and Gordon almost started to celebrate, but I cut the party short.

"But," my index finger was raised, "there'll have to be some rules."

"Just name 'em." Curt was beaming, and I almost backed down, until memories of my little brother's childhood bedroom resurfaced in my mind, complete with smell-o-vision.

"Well, first of all, you're going to have to be responsible for yourself—your food, your laundry, your messes."

Curt was nodding. "That's cool."

I continued. "You're welcome to eat meals with us as long as you can chip in on the groceries and take turns cooking."

"No problem," Curt replied. "I make a mean macaroni and cheese, and Mom taught me how to make french toast last year."

Gordon was looking at me now. "So you'll give the basketball tryouts a go?"

I placed my elbow on the table and rested my chin in my hand. "I haven't played competitive ball in over two years. I'm just not sure if I'm good enough."

Surprisingly, it was my little brother's next comment that rang true. "Molly, I bet I've seen every single basketball game you've ever played in. You were never the tallest or fastest out there. And you haven't always been the best player on the court. But I've never seen you give less than your very best, and that was always enough. I'm sure it still is."

At that moment I wanted nothing more than to stand up and give my younger brother a great big sisterly hug. But before I even had a chance, he held up his empty plate. "Can I have seconds?"

Chapter
THREE

In a matter of twenty-four hours we had transformed our office into a humble bedroom for my brother. This wasn't exactly how I had envisioned the transition from two to three would occur in our family unit. I'd pictured diapers and *Sesame Street*, not boxer shorts and ESPN. But Curt and Gordon were convinced that this was a great situation for all of us. I, on the other hand, wasn't so sure.

One perk with this arrangement, however, was that my little brother suddenly became my self-appointed coach during the week before basketball tryouts. The kid was actually a pretty good ball player, and knew muscles, and how to train them to achieve a peak performance, like Ronald McDonald knows French fries.

The two of us got up early and ran every day before classes—something I often did anyway but found it nice to have a partner. In the evenings, when Gordon was at work, Curt and I would shoot hoops in the Kendall's driveway. It wasn't an ideal situation, but the weather was nice, the driveway was level, and the hoop was at regulation height. It would have to do.

On Friday evening, after I managed to stomp my brother in a friendly game of one-on-one, we both collapsed on the Kendall's lawn in an attempt to cool down.

"Molly, I have no doubt you're going to rock the house tomorrow at your tryouts." Curt pulled off his white T-shirt and was now using it to absorb the sweat from his face and the back of his neck.

"I think I'll just settle for not being totally laughed right out of the gym by the coach and other players." As I spoke, I wiped my own glistening face with the back of my arm.

I had no sooner dropped my arm when my little brother's sweat-drenched shirt flew into my face before falling to the grass.

"Hey, watch it," I hollered, while attempting to hurl the foul-smelling T-shirt back into Curt's face. He was too quick and caught it in his hands.

"Molly, you're such a dweeb. Didn't you notice? You totally kicked my butt tonight!"

"Yeah, well I'm going to kick it again if that shirt lands in my face one more time."

"I surrender. I surrender." Curt laughed and held up the shirt again, this time waving it in the air.

"Put that thing down. You're making me nervous."

"You have no reason to be nervous. You're going to do great tomorrow."

"That's not exactly what I was referring to." I reached for the basketball on the grass and held it up in front of me. "But now that you mention it, I am nervous about the tryouts tomorrow."

"Just do the same things that you did here tonight. The coach would be a fool to cut you from the tryouts." Now Curt was pointing his finger at me. "You're good, Molly. And I'm not just saying that because I noticed a plate of homemade chocolate chip cookies on top of the fridge."

Some things—like my little brother's voracious appetite—never change. "My visiting teachers brought the cookies by today."

"And are you going to share them with a growing boy?"

I raised my eyebrows while sizing up my sandy blonde haired, six-foot two-inch kid brother and wondered for a moment if he ever *would* quit growing. The guy had probably added two inches in height and twenty pounds of muscle in just the past year alone.

"I guess for all your hard work and pep talks over the past week you at least deserve a cookie. How about we eat a little dinner first, though?" I knew I was sounding a bit like a mother hen, but for some reason, I was feeling a little maternal when it came to my brother's well-being. I wondered if these feelings were natural because I didn't recall ever having them when we lived under the same roof growing up. Back in those days, he was more of an annoyance to me than anything.

After dinner, I went straight to bed but not to sleep (I always read before turning out the lights). As usual, Gordon was working the late shift at the grocery store and wouldn't get home until I was already asleep. I was a little frustrated that I wouldn't see him until after the tryouts. I really wished he were here to offer some moral support because, if I was honest with myself, I was a little more than nervous about these basketball tryouts—I was completely terrified.

❈❈❈

When I walked into the Reed Gym at 8 A.M. on Saturday morning it took approximately 3.2 seconds for my instincts (or insecurities) to kick in and tell me I'd made a huge mistake. Why was I even here? Who did I think I was, trying out for a college basketball team when I hadn't played competitively for two whole years?

Given another 3.2 seconds to carefully ponder the entire situation, I was no longer irritated with myself. I was irritated with Gordon and Curt. Why had I let them talk me into this?

A girl wearing shorts and a T-shirt and carrying a clipboard approached me.

She sounded quite uninterested as she spoke. "Are you here for the tryouts?"

"Yep," I replied.

Regret began to assault me the minute I spoke. *Why* had I said that? It would have been just as easy to say, "No," "Nope," "Not me," or even, "Not a chance." The clipboard girl asked my name and wrote it down. Now I was committed.

She then handed me some sort of questionnaire along with a pencil and instructed me to fill it out as quickly as possible before we got started. Four other girls were sitting on the bleachers, presumably filling out the same form, so I found a spot on the wooden bench and began answering the questions—mostly about my background with basketball.

I was glad I could write down that I was a starter on the Oakley Jr. High and High School basketball teams, but I'd graduated over two years ago. I still looked young, though. Maybe the coach wouldn't notice the dates. Right! And I doubted that my one hundred percent victory margin over Gordon in the game of Horse would count.

As I was filling out the form, ten girls—or should I say women, perhaps even Amazons—began running some basic drills. At least half of them were a good six feet or taller. At five foot eight, I was feeling a little like Tinkerbell—quite the new sensation. Under the circumstances, I wasn't sure that I liked it.

After a few more minutes, a man wearing a baseball cap walked to the center of the court and blew a whistle that was hanging from a string around his neck. All of the women that were warming up, as well as those on the bleachers began to migrate toward him. I followed along.

Clipboard Girl, who I assumed must be an assistant coach, walked up to Whistle Guy, obviously the coach, and handed him the roster as well as our questionnaires.

After examining his clipboard, the coach finally spoke. "I'm so glad you all showed up this morning. I'm Russ Hill, head coach of the Lady Bengals. You can call me Coach.

"I assume you all know there are only two positions open for the team this year. Don't let this discourage you."

I almost expected to hear a collective groan from the others vying for the two coveted walk-on positions. But aside from some heavy breathing by those who had just been running drills, the gym was eerily quiet.

The coach continued. "I have five returning players this year and five new players that I've recruited. By the end of our practice today I hope to have an idea of who else will join the team. Good luck, ladies."

The coach blew his whistle again (what is it about coaches and whistles anyway?) and instructed us to stand on the line at one side of the court and run sprints back and forth. During the first few sprints, I was grateful I'd continued running several times a week, even after I'd finished my sports career at Oakley High School. But after number four or five, I wondered why I hadn't trained a little harder. This was a killer.

After finishing the sprints, as well as several passing and shooting drills, Clipboard Girl, who was actually named Deb, brought out red and white, sleeveless, mesh jerseys and we were split into teams for a scrimmage. I must admit, however, I was a little relieved to be sitting out at first. It would be nice to observe the competition without the pressure of performing. It also gave me a chance to catch my breath.

As I found a spot on the bench, one of the team's secured players sat down next to me. Her long brunette hair was pulled up high into a ponytail and braided, leaving only a wisp of bangs free to fall across her forehead. She wasn't wearing makeup and had obviously been blessed with the clear complexion and dark lashes I only dreamed about every day when I applied foundation and mascara.

"You've handled the ball quite a bit, I can tell," she said. I looked over both of my shoulders before I realized she was talking to me.

"I played in high school. How about you?" I asked.

"Four years at Jenks High School in Tulsa, Oklahoma."

"Really? My husband's from Tulsa."

"Your husband? You mean you're *married?*" By the look on her face, you'd have thought I'd told her I was an exchange student from Siberia—or maybe Saturn.

"If you don't mind my asking, how old are you?"

"Twenty."

"No way! I figured you were a freshman, like me."

I wondered if she was trying to make me feel old, because it really wasn't necessary. The sprints had already achieved that task quite successfully.

The whistle blew again, and this time I heard my name. "Amy, Molly, on the court."

We both hopped off the bench, and for the next hour (with a few breaks here and there) we played some serious hoops. I hadn't experienced this type of competition since regional playoffs my senior year. This was intense, and I was loving every sweaty, fingernail-breaking, muscle-straining minute of it. I hadn't played at BYU-Idaho because there wasn't a team. I'd forgotten just how much I enjoyed this game.

Once again, the coach blew his whistle. I figured he was switching out players again.

"That'll be it for today, ladies. You can go ahead and get showered up, except for those trying out for the team today. If you five would come over here and take a seat on the bleachers for just a minute, I'll announce my decision."

As I approached the bench my stomach felt like it was full of rocks, and my heart was beating faster than during the sprints. After spending the morning rediscovering my love for a sport I'd simply forgotten about—or at least how much I enjoyed it—I wanted one of the spots on this team more than I wanted all the boxes of fudge-covered Oreos in the entire state of Idaho.

"First, I'd like to thank you all. This was a tough workout today, ladies, and you all did a wonderful job. Unfortunately we have only two positions available."

The coach paused for a bit, and just when I was about to stand up and shake his shoulders, he made his announcement.

"So I've decided to give these spots to Kim Jensen and Molly Nelson."

It took every ounce of self-control to contain my excitement as I accepted congratulations from three very disappointed girls and, finally, shared a brief embrace with Kim. I wanted to scream and shout and run around with my fists raised in the air as if I'd won an Olympic gold medal. Instead, I settled for a huge grin.

Coach Hill interrupted my thoughts. "I hold practice right here from 4:30 to 6, Monday through Thursday. I'll see you two back here Monday afternoon."

I was so excited I didn't even bother to shower. There'd be time for that later. All I could think about at the moment was getting home and thanking a couple of crazy guys for talking me into something I didn't even realize I wanted to do.

Chapter
FOUR

One of the nice things about attending Idaho State University in Pocatello is that we're only an hour and fifteen minutes away from my hometown of Oakley; far enough to be on our own but close enough to enjoy one of Mom's famous roast-beef-with-mashed-potatoes-and-gravy Sunday dinners when you just need a good home-cooked meal.

As a newlywed, the more time I spend in the kitchen attempting to create things suitable for the palate (i.e., something that would go down and stay down), the more I realize just how miraculous and wonderful my mother's cooking skills truly are. I'm sure Gordon was in awe of her culinary skills as well. And the poor guy could only hope and pray (and suffer in silence) that such attributes were somehow hereditary—or eventually contagious.

But before feasting on Mom's Sunday meal masterpiece, we did what the Chambers family has always done on Sunday mornings, since before I was born. We attended church together—an aspect of my life that I'm not sure I always appreciated growing up but more and more have found a sense of peace and wholeness in.

It was nice to see so many familiar faces and say hello to old friends in my home ward. After Relief Society, which was the first meeting in our three hour session, a few sisters gravitated in my general direction while I was attempting to exit the room.

Sister Henning, my Beehive advisor from a million years ago, wrapped her right arm around my shoulder and pulled me in close, while clutching the handle of a plastic baby carrier with her left. It looked like the same baby—and same baby carrier—that she had toted around way back then. "Oh, Molly, I just can't believe you're all grown up and married."

"Well, I still wonder about the 'grown-up' part, but yeah, it's been four months now."

Sister Gleason, who probably taught every one of us Chamber kids in Primary (and will forever be immortalized in the Primary Teacher Hall of Fame due to her weekly treat distribution amongst her happy—and hyper—students), leaned over to add her own thought to our conversation.

"I was three months pregnant by the time Lee and I had been married four months. And can you believe I didn't even realize it! I thought I had some bad case of the flu." She leaned in even closer and lowered her voice. "Nothing, and I mean not even *saltines*, would stay down, it was that bad. I spent a good three months in the bathroom, or with my face in a bucket. Not exactly an ideal situation for a newlywed."

Wow. Now that was more information than I ever really wanted to know about Sister Gleasen. I had been completely happy—if not somewhat ignorant—with this fine woman's image engraved in my memory as the "treat teacher." Now, I would forever envision my beloved primary teacher heaped over the toilet seat losing her crackers. Disturbing!

Now it was Sister Henning's turn. "Our Joshua, who's a Deacon now, was a honeymoon baby. And when he came five weeks premature I could just see the people at church doing the math in their heads."

Both sisters chuckled and I suddenly had the creepy feeling that every woman passing by our little "pregnancy horror story" conversation was checking out my stomach for the slightest hint of a bulge. I was forever grateful that I hadn't put on any weight—whether caused by pregnancy or Pringles—over the past four months.

By the time Sacrament meeting ended and we had reached the car, I'd probably heard the phrase, "How's married life?" in one variation or another approximately eleven times, as well as at least four references to pregnancy or babies (including the scene after Relief Society). I guess I understood the fascination, but at times it felt a bit intrusive. We were simply newlyweds, not tabloid celebrities.

❈❈❈

The minute we walked into the house after church, I knew we'd made a magnificent decision to spend the day in Oakley. The succulent aroma of slowly cooked roast beef spontaneously induced a round of "mmmms" and we all involuntarily began to practice deep breathing exercises through the nose. Coincidence? I think not!

Gordon and I quickly changed out of our church clothes and into jeans and T-shirts (typical student attire) and made our way back to the kitchen to help put the finishing touches on dinner. Mom was still in her dress but wearing an apron now.

To top off the wonder of the entire Sunday dinner experience at the Chambers household, my mother knew how to prepare and time meals so they cooked while we were gone, and were ready within a half hour after arriving home. Forget about an enrichment night mini-class., the woman deserved her own cooking show on PBS.

When we were all finally seated, and the blessing had been asked, my youngest brother Dusty (our current Oakley High School football star) was the first to speak; the rest of us were too preoccupied with piling our plates full of food.

"You guys need to visit every weekend. For the past couple of weeks all we've had for Sunday dinner is leftovers."

Curt was quick to intervene. "Just be grateful you have Mom's leftovers. At least you know they'll taste good. Up until a week ago, I was surviving on PB&J, Lucky Charms, and basically anything frozen or from a can that could be nuked in the microwave and edible within a few minutes."

Now it was Dad's turn. "And how are things going with the three of you living in the Nelson residence?"

"Some honeymoon," Dusty said with a chuckle.

"Are you two sure this is a good arrangement?" Mom said, directing her question toward me and Gordon.

Curt responded before I even had a chance. "It works for me."

Dad picked up a warm dinner roll and tossed it at Curt. "I don't think Mom was talking to you. Besides, anything works for you, son, as long as you have food in your stomach and a television nearby."

Curt mumbled something inaudible, while nodding, since he'd already taken a huge bite from the soft roll.

Gordon was quick to defend our new living arrangements. "Actually, I feel a little better knowing that Molly doesn't have to be alone every evening while I'm at work. And since Curt's helping out with the rent, Molly can quit her job at the bookstore and focus on her classes and basketball."

"I still can't believe I made the team," I said, mostly because I wanted to change the direction of the conversation. Sometimes Mom and Dad tended to worry just a little too much.

"That's so wonderful, honey," Mom said, while passing the gravy to Dad. "You always loved basketball in high school."

"She's still really good, too," Curt chimed in. It was good to have his support.

"It's all relative," I replied. "Some of those girls are incredibly talented—and tall. I'm still not sure why the coach picked me."

"Oh, I'm sure you'll do just wonderful," said Mom. I could have told the woman I was taking up spelunking, or even sponge collecting, and her response would have been the same. As long as I wasn't doing something illegal, immoral, or incredibly dangerous, she has always been my biggest cheerleader.

Mom continued, this time focusing her comment to Curt. "I saw you talking to the bishop today. What was that about?"

Curt took another bite of his roll and spoke with his mouth full. "He was asking me if I was still planning to serve a mission."

This simple statement seemed to capture everyone's attention.

"And . . . ?" Dad queried.

"I told him, 'yeah.'" Curt dug his spoon into a mound of mashed potatoes as he spoke.

I happened to notice an exchanged look of relief between Mom and Dad. This was definitely good news. Curt has always been a good kid—never into any serious trouble—but during his senior year of high school he seemed to be struggling with his testimony. Of course, this was all hearsay from Mom. I'd never really sat down and talked about it with my little brother. Now that he was living with me and Gordon, I was certain the subject would come up.

"When do you turn nineteen?" Gordon asked.

"Not 'till spring," Curt replied.

"April 28th, to be exact," I clarified.

Curt pointed his spoon at Gordon. "You went on a mission, right?"

"Best two years of my life." Gordon replied. "Well, up until I met a certain strawberry blonde. I'm afraid your sister ruined me—a good kind of ruin, if you know what I mean—and I knew I'd either have to marry her, or flee to Tibet and become a monk. I'm just glad it all worked out; I don't do well at high altitudes, and I'm pretty sure I'd look silly as a bald guy."

Dad looked at me while pointing to Gordon. "Now, where did you find this guy?"

"He asked me to dance one day. I said "yes," and next thing I knew, I had a ring on my finger."

Gordon put his finger to the side of his face and took on a contemplative expression. "Hmmmm . . . I seem to remember a little more to the story. Like having to win your heart over from a certain Brandon Mace, high school heartthrob and returned missionary extraordinaire."

I looked into Gordon's blue eyes. "Brandon never had my heart." I'm afraid I sounded a bit defensive.

Gordon raised an eyebrow.

"I swear, he didn't have my heart. He had two years worth of letters from his mission, and maybe a blood vessel or an artery, but not my heart."

Gordon simply smiled.

Oh, how I loved that smile—and the man that went with it.

Chapter
FIVE

Basketball practice began on Monday, and even though I was no longer working at the bookstore, life was still incredibly hectic. All of my classes had kicked into high gear and I was doing my best to hold on for the ride.

My new schedule also brought on a physical challenge I hadn't expected. I thought since my athletic days of high school I'd stayed in pretty good shape through regular jogging as well as taking a dance class at BYU–Idaho.

Boy, was I wrong.

Being a new member of the Lady Bengals, I was exerting my physical limits in a way I'd never before experienced. I ached in places I didn't even think could ache. And I wasn't the only one.

"I feel like I've been thrown from a Brahma bull and then trampled a few times over," Amy, my teammate from Tulsa, commented as the two of us were leaving practice on Wednesday and heading out to the parking lot of the Reed Gym. Ever since we met on the first day of tryouts, the two of us tended to gravitate toward one another during the slower moments of practice.

I stretched my arms into the mild fall air and then winced as my weary muscles responded to the recent workout. "I'm wondering if maybe I'm just too old for all of this."

"Well, Grandma," Amy said with a sly grin, "you seem to be holding your own out on the court. I can't believe it's been two years since you played competitively."

"Actually, me either," I replied. "Honestly, the past two years have passed by so fast and so much in my life has changed. Sometimes, when I stop and think about it all, I'm a little blown away."

"Really? Why?"

"I guess I'm just amazed that within such a short period of time I could fall in love—and with the person that I probably least expected."

Amy's eyes grew big. "Oh, I've *got* to hear this. I'm such a sucker for a good love story."

"How about I tell you over a bowl of homemade soup?"

"You're domestic too? I'm impressed."

"Actually, no," I replied. "But I decided to break in one of the three Crock-Pots we received as wedding gifts. It came with a recipe book called *Crock-Pot Cooking for Dummies*. I may not be a great chef, but I *do* know how to follow instructions."

"Hey, the only thing I love more than a good love story is when someone feeds me while telling me a good love story."

Since Amy was on foot, we drove Old Blue, my ancient truck that still somehow managed to get me from here to there, up the hill to our humble basement apartment.

When I opened the door leading down to our apartment, I expected the scent of stewing onion, garlic, and chicken to greet me, similar to the experience of walking into Mom's kitchen on Sunday afternoons.

But, instead of smelling the tender morsels of my Crock-Pot creation, I could pick up the faint odor of burnt bacon, mixed with what could only be smelly socks: a scent that had been engraved within my nostrils years earlier while being raised in a family of four athletic brothers.

With trepidation, I slowly walked down the stairs, unsure of what I might find. The further I descended, the stronger the stench became. I was so caught up in this unexpected odor situation, I forgot that Amy was following close behind.

When I finally reached the bottom of the stairs and entered the living area, I couldn't help but notice a few mounds of clothes—obviously dirty—in separate piles on the floor in front of the couch. One consisted of whites, while another was made up of blue jeans, and another had a blend of colored clothes. I also noticed that the television was tuned into what must have been a rugby game. Dirty dishes were sitting on the coffee table, but the couch—the only place to sit in the room besides the table and chairs—was empty.

Now, I'm definitely not the queen of housekeeping; never in my life have I been obsessive about cleanliness and order. But I'm not a total slobazoid either. I've always drawn the line when noxious odors are involved. My sinuses are just way too sensitive to deal with stink. The current situation in my apartment was beyond my tolerance level.

Another thing was certain: Gordon wasn't involved with any of this. The guy could hardly open a week-old food container in the fridge without the smell triggering his gag reflex. He was worse than me. Besides, he'd been on campus all day either attending class, studying, or tutoring.

No, I knew who the messy, stinky culprit was, and when I found him . . .

With clenched fists—and only breathing through my mouth for obvious reasons—I was about to take a step into the "toxic-sock zone" when Curt entered from the hallway wearing nothing but the little plaid blanket I'd always kept on the back of the couch in case my feet got cold while I was watching TV. It was wrapped around his bottom half and slightly resembled a kilt.

"Whoa," Curt hollered as he came to an abrupt stop. "Molly, I didn't hear you come in." Then he looked over at Amy and folded his arms in front of him, obviously realizing his lack of clothes.

"So where are the bagpipes to go with your little outfit?" I couldn't resist asking, as I once again appraised my brother's choice of wardrobe. My little remark also minimized the likelihood that I might bite my little brother's head off at any moment.

Curt looked down at his "clothes" and chuckled. "Oh, you mean this." He held out the edges of his "kilt" like a little girl would if she were about to curtsey. "Actually, I got mustard all over my only clean shorts. I accidentally dropped part of my bacon sandwich when the blue team scored."

Typical Curt! The kid would watch any athletic event he could find. He was a sports-a-holic. It didn't matter that he knew nothing about a particular sport or team—he just loved a good battle. Well, he was about to get one.

"You don't have any other clean clothes?" I asked but then looked at the smelling color-coded mounds on the ground and held up my hand. "Oh, silly me! Of course you don't have any clean clothes. They're in piles all over the floor." Now I raised my voice.

"I was about to do my laundry—I haven't done any since I left Oakley—but you're out of laundry detergent."

It was at this point that Amy spoke up, and to be honest, I'd almost forgotten that she was even there because I was so furious with my brother.

"Maybe I'd just better head on home, Molly. We can hang out and eat soup another time."

"No, please stay. I'm sure Curt's going to pick up his dirty clothes any minute. Besides, I can't eat this Crock-Pot full of soup all by myself."

"Uh-oh." Curt slapped his hand to his forehead.

I almost didn't want to ask. "What?"

"I forgot to plug that crock-thingy back in."

"You unplugged it?" Now I really was yelling.

"It was just going to be for a few minutes while I made toast this morning." My brother looked sheepish, and he was about to get slaughtered.

"Curt, I'm going to *kill* you!" I screamed as I headed into our narrow kitchen. "That was supposed to be our dinner and now it's probably spoiled."

Amy poked her head around the kitchen corner. "Really, Molly, I'm sure you and your husband don't need me around right now. We can do this another time. And, anyway, I have a ton of homework waiting back at the dorm."

After Amy spoke, Curt and I looked at each other for a good three seconds before we both began to laugh.

"Did I say something funny?" Amy asked.

"More scary than funny," I replied with a chuckle. "Actually, Curt's my brother, *not* my husband." I almost shuddered at the thought.

A visual wave of relief and understanding washed over Amy's expression.

I continued my explanation. "He moved in with me and Gordon—my husband—last week. Curt's a freshman here at ISU, too."

I noticed an awkward exchange between Amy and Curt and realized that as mad as I was at my little brother right now, I certainly couldn't deny him a proper introduction to a beautiful young lady like Amy. Of course, he didn't make the situation easy dressed up like some psychotic, Scottish rugby fan.

"I'm sorry, I'll try to forget for a moment that I'm *furious* with my little brother and introduce you two. Curt, this is my teammate Amy. She's from Tulsa, Oklahoma." Now I gestured to my brother. "Amy, this is my brother, Curt, who normally doesn't dress in a skirt, mess up my house, and ruin my dinner."

My little brother simply ignored the hostility evident in my voice and held out his hand. "Nice to meet you, Amy."

Amy smiled back at him and I noticed a little glint in her eye as the two exchanged glances and shook hands. "Nice to meet you too. Is it Curt?"

My brother nodded, smiling, and I couldn't help notice that, aside from his little get-up, the guy really was what most girls would consider "hot." He'd spent much of the summer out in the fields with Dad and the sun left its mark on both his hair and skin. If you didn't know he was from Idaho, you might even think he was from the California beach.

And then, there were the muscles—Curt had an abundance of them. They were quite a sight, and presently on display in my kitchen. The kid may not have been diligent about keeping up with his laundry, but he never missed a day working out.

I grabbed a dish towel that was draped on a hook and snapped it at a particularly impressive bicep. "Come here, kiddo. You're not exactly the same size, but I bet Gordon has some sweats and a T-shirt you can wear until you get your laundry done. Then Amy and I can have a gourmet dinner of chicken-flavored ramen noodles."

"Sounds good to me," Amy remarked with a smile on her face. I highly doubted she was grinning at the thought of eating a ten-cent package of flavored noodles with her teammate.

Chapter
SIX

When my alarm clock sounded at six-thirty in the morning, I wanted nothing more than to turn it off, snuggle up next to Gordon, and fall back asleep for a few more hours. Even though my husband was practically comatose (the guy worked way too hard), these moments together were cherished. Aside from weekends, it seemed like the six precious hours—twelve-thirty to six-thirty— were all the time we ever spent together lately—even though we were asleep.

My reality, however, was that a big, ugly quiz was waiting for me in my eight o'clock economics class, ready and eager to suck a mass of crammed information from my overloaded brain. I had no choice but to drag myself out of bed, wander into the shower, and hope that after a few minutes of water pounding on my face, I'd somehow come alive. It usually worked.

When I turned on the bathroom light and looked into the mirror after my eyes had adjusted, I was surprised to see my face framed in a huge heart drawn in red-lipstick. Across the top of the mirror was written *Hello beautiful* and at the bottom it read *No, this message is NOT for you, Curt!*

I looked at my reflection—rumpled hair and puffy eyes smudged with the remnants of black mascara—and smiled. *He thinks I'm beautiful?* I couldn't help but chuckle and send a little prayer heavenward, thanking Father for bringing Gordon Nelson into my life.

The partially used tube of red lipstick was sitting on the side of the bathroom sink and one thing was for sure: it didn't belong to me. Gordon must have concocted this idea while stocking the make-up aisle last night at the grocery store.

A wonderful idea suddenly sprang into my mind. After applying an ample amount of "Ruby Red" to my lips, I tiptoed back into our bedroom and placed a very gentle and very red kiss onto the cheek of my sleeping husband.

Gordon stirred under the covers and mumbled something inaudible. Maybe he was trying to say, "Love you," but I couldn't be sure. It came out more like a moan.

When I returned to the bathroom and glanced back into the mirror, I actually laughed out loud but then covered my mouth to control the noise. What a fright! If Gordon could see my face right now, he'd definitely question his previous assessment of my beauty. I looked like either a very tired vampire, or a little kid who had just consumed an entire box of cherry-flavored popsicles.

In my best lipstickmanship I wrote *Back at ya, handsome!* and hopped into the shower, praying that "Ruby Red" would wash off. I really couldn't go to class looking like I'd just puckered up to a freshly painted barn.

Curt, who also had an eight o'clock class—and thank goodness agreed to shower at night—was sitting in front of the TV eating a bowl of some colorful cereal while watching water polo.

"Morning," he said with his mouth full.

"Do you ever watch anything besides sports?" I asked.

Curt looked thoughtful for a moment. "I like Jeopardy."

"I think you like any type of competition."

Curt simply shrugged and returned his attention back to water polo, so I made my way to the kitchen in search of something I could call breakfast.

Halfway to the kitchen my brother's voice caught my attention. "Hey, sorry again about yesterday. You know, my dirty laundry all over and unplugging your soup maker thingy." Curt truly looked sincere. How could I hold a grudge?

"It's called a Crock-Pot and don't worry about it. Stuff happens."

"Yeah, well, next time 'stuff happens' I'd like to avoid the ever so convincing slobbish fool impression. Especially in front of a beautiful girl like Amy." Curt sighed before heaping another spoonful of cereal into his mouth.

I grabbed a banana on the counter and walked over to the couch. "Didn't you notice?" I asked as I sat down next to my brother, peeling my breakfast.

Curt looked puzzled. "Notice what?"

"The look in Amy's eyes." Sheesh, the guy was clueless.

"Well, it's kind of hard to be perceptive in front of a beautiful woman when you're wearing a skirt."

"Honestly, Curt, I don't think she noticed what you were wearing as much as she noticed your charm and good looks."

"Oh, right. Excuse me while I go laugh my skirt off!"

I nearly choked on a bite of banana and had to take a swig of Curt's orange juice before I could continue. "I'm serious. And I think I know just a little bit about women."

Curt put his bowl down on the coffee table and turned to face me. "So, if you're right, how can I get to know this Amy girl a little better?"

"How about you show up after basketball practice. You know, the thoughtful younger brother escorting his sister home."

"Wouldn't I look a little conspicuous if I suddenly started showing up at your practices?"

"Curt, any girl in her right mind would be completely thrilled if you went out of your way to see her. I doubt it would even matter if you used the excuse of escorting your sister home."

Curt leaned his back against the couch cushion. "Okay, I'll trust your judgment, Molly. But I just don't want to end up looking like a fool again."

I put my hand on my brother's strong shoulder. "Trust me," I said and resisted the urge to pat myself on my matchmaking back.

※※※

That afternoon, when I arrived at my noon American Literature class with maybe a minute to spare, I was surprised to see the other students leaving with a piece of paper in their hands. After making my way into the room, a student aid from the English department handed me one of the papers. I was about to ask what it was, but she didn't give me a chance.

"Dr. Gardner had an emergency and has canceled his classes for the day. This is a take-home quiz. It's due back next class. Oh, and you can use your books."

Score! Any time there was a take-home quiz where you could use your book, it was definitely a time to rejoice. And to top it off, no class. Woohoo!

Since Gordon would still be tutoring at the math lab, I decided to go over and hang around for a half-hour. I was pretty sure he got off at 12:30 and would have just enough time to skarf down a PB&J, or whatever he'd brought for his lunch, before heading to his 1 P.M. class. Both of our schedules were so crazy, I was certain he'd find my presence a big surprise.

When I showed up at the math lab and peered into the window, I noticed Gordon leaning over a rather large, muscular fellow with blonde hair. Gordon pointed to the guy's textbook and then began punching numbers into his calculator. After a few moments the two began to chuckle and my husband patted the guy on the back. I couldn't begin to imagine what bit of humor these two found in anything related to math, but Gordon had a gift for exposing the lighter side to any situation. It was a talent that I almost always appreciated—unless I just really wanted to be mad and wallow in self-pity. Then I found it irritating.

Something about the guy he was tutoring seemed vaguely familiar, but since I could only see the top of his head and part of his face, it was hard to tell. He was probably in one of my classes, or maybe I'd seen him when I was working at the bookstore.

Gordon still had twenty minutes left of tutoring and since he wasn't expecting me, I figured I'd peek in and tell him I was waiting outside. Then, maybe I'd find a nice spot against the wall and get some reading done.

When I entered the lab, the room was quiet except for the lowered voices of the tutors as they circled the room giving instruction to those in need. After shutting the door softly behind me, I made my way across the room to where my husband stood.

"Hey," I whispered, placing a hand on his shoulder.

When Gordon turned to face me, his blue eyes lit up in surprise and a smile spread across his face. "What are you doing here? I thought you had American Lit at noon."

"I do, but it was canceled," I replied. "So, I was thinking that maybe I'd stop in and visit for a few minutes."

"Sure," Gordon said as he looked up at the clock. "But I don't finish here for another fifteen minutes or so."

I let my hand slide down Gordon's arm until it reached his hand where it found a welcoming squeeze. "I'll just be waiting out in the hall—reading."

"Sounds good," Gordon whispered and leaned over to give me a brief kiss on the lips. Oh, how I loved Gordon's kisses—even the brief ones.

A deep and somewhat familiar voice interrupted our little romantic exchange. "Hey, Gordon, do you kiss all the pretty girls that come in here looking for a little help with their math?"

Gordon and I quickly parted and a chuckle escaped my husband's mouth before he spoke. "Chad, this is my wife, Molly. Molly, this is Chad. He's a regular here. You know those football players. They have no problem lining up dates or plowing down linebackers, but give them a linear equation and they're practically helpless." Gordon smiled and patted his friend on the back.

Any feelings of bliss I was experiencing instantly vanished as I found myself looking directly into the face of probably the only person on earth that I could honestly say I truly hated.

"Molly." Just the sound of his voice saying my name made me sick. *Everything* about Chad Hanks made me sick.

Gordon looked from me to Chad and then back to me again. Obviously, he sensed the friction. "I take it you two know each other."

"Yeah," *unfortunately!* "Chad's from Oakley. We went to high school together." I wanted to add that Chad was the biggest jerk this side of Jupiter. Not only did he briefly date my cousin and best friend Shannon when he was a senior and she was a sophomore, but the guy—or should I say wolf—got her pregnant and then basically abandoned her and any responsibility with the pregnancy because he had more important aspirations for his future, like becoming a hotshot college football star.

Shannon placed the baby (a little girl) up for adoption, but her struggles from one not-so-little mistake lingered for years—*still* linger, even though her life has turned around. She now has a temple marriage to Justin Collins, a great guy, and the two live in Rexburg. She had finally moved beyond the memory of Chad Hanks and the mess he left her in. And now, here I was face-to-face with the guy who most women find incredibly attractive. All he did for me was make me want to throw up.

Chad half smiled as he spoke, "High school seems like another lifetime ago."

"Yeah, well, for some of us it's an all-too-recent memory or nightmare." I stated flatly. Then, not wanting to further the conversation with this demon from my cousin's past, I turned to Gordon. "Actually, I'm pretty tired. I think I'm just going to head on home, get some lunch, and take a nap. I'll see you later." Without waiting for his response, I headed for the door, relieved to have Chad Hanks behind me.

Chapter
SEVEN

"Hey, Molly, wait up."

I turned around, my eyes searching the mass of migrating students for the face attached to that familiar female voice. It only took a few seconds before I caught sight of the waving hand and warm smile. My teammate, Amy, had quickly become a dear friend. We both had a freakishly similar sense of humor (that some would even call quirky), as well as a love of basketball and chocolate (not necessarily in that order). What more could you ask for in a friend?

When Amy finally reached me, her carefree expression turned to one of concern. "Are you okay? You look upset." That was an understatement. I'd just encountered my husband having an innocent little chuckle with Chad Hanks—creep extraordinaire. I guess it was inevitable that I'd encounter the guy at some point since we were both students at Idaho State University. But to be honest, I'd long forgotten he was a student and football player here.

I wasn't in the mood to talk about, let alone think about, Chad Hanks, so I tried to paste on a smile and change the subject.

"I'm just tired; it's already been a long day."

"I hear ya," Amy replied.

"So, where are you headed?" I asked.

"Back to the dorms," Amy said with a sigh about as heavy as the overloaded backpack slung across her shoulder.

"Ahhh, dorm life. I remember it well. But as much as I loved my roommates, I think I prefer sharing The Cave with Gordon and Curt. Well, except for when Curt attempts to do his laundry."

"Yeah, well at least you have roommates you can laugh with. Or in the case of Curt, laugh at." Amy's eyes gave a playful twinkle when she mentioned my brother's name. "Somehow, I was paired up with Dana from some place called Mud Lake. The girl hates sports, including basketball, and loves eighties music, crossword puzzles which must be done in silence—at least I get a break from the eighties music—and dill pickles. I *hate* dill pickles. I hate *any* pickles. I wanna heave when my nose picks up even the slightest hint of pickle fumes."

I laughed at Amy's description. "Pickle fumes?"

"Honestly, Molly, I'm trying to be a trooper, but I'm not sure I'm going to survive the semester with the girl from Mud Lake."

"What are your options, aside from cultivating a love for hamburger relish?" I asked.

"I don't have any," she replied. "Since my scholarship included room and board in the dorms, I'll just have to deal with Miss Pickle. I suppose I could pay rent somewhere else out of my own pocket, but, well, they seem to be a bit empty these days." Amy patted her pockets.

"I hear ya. The things we put ourselves through so we can shoot some hoops. The only reason Curt is living with us is because he helps with the rent so I can play on the team."

When I mentioned Curt's name, I noticed a grin make its way onto Amy's face.

"What's that for?" I asked, even though I already knew.

"What's what for?" Amy countered.

"The grin. You know, that thing that nearly splits your face in two any time my brother's name is mentioned."

"I'm just a happy person," Amy responded. "Well, when I don't have to smell pickles or listen to Boy George songs."

I decided not to push the subject about Curt, but another thought entered my head. "What ya doing this weekend?"

"I've got *big plans*," Amy replied. "I have a few hot dates: biology tonight and Spanish tomorrow. I might even squeeze in dinner with my humanities book."

"Sounds entirely too exciting."

"And when I'm not studying," Amy continued, "I plan on vegging out in front of my TV. Thank goodness for earphones. It's the only way I'm surviving Dana's music. Hey, maybe I should try nose plugs for the pickle fumes—or a gas mask."

"How'd you like to go the entire weekend without worrying about your pickle fumes, nose plugs, or Boy George."

Amy raised an eyebrow. "I'm listening."

"Why don't you come with us back home to Oakley this week-end? It's Homecoming so we're talking a little football action, a little Monopoly action, and a lot of my Mom's good cooking. We'll head back to Pocatello sometime Sunday, after church."

At first Amy looked excited, but at the mention of church, a dubious expression seemed to shroud her previous enthusiasm. "I haven't been to church in a million years, Molly. The building may just fall down if I walk through its doors."

"Oh, please!" I wailed. "I seriously doubt that. Plus, our church building is made of bricks. Haven't you ever heard of the three little pigs?"

Amy groaned. "Okay, if you're willing to risk it. But I won't be held responsible for any damage."

"We'll take our chances." I replied.

Amy was quiet for a moment and I could see a bit of reticence in her eyes, but she finally spoke her mind. "Molly, you're not going to try to turn me into a Mormon, are you?"

"Not if you don't want to."

"Whew. Okay. And don't worry, I'll let you know if I change my mind and decide to sign up."

"Sounds like a plan. But you might have to remind me to leave my scriptures at home while we're at the football game. I get a little overzealous sometimes."

Amy nudged my shoulder with hers in a playful manner. "So, when do we leave?"

❊❊❊

The drive to Oakley flew by as Gordon, Curt, Amy, and I reminisced about high school horror stories; from peculiar prom dates to cafeteria chaos—collectively, we'd experienced it all. A fun aspect of the conversation was that Amy and Gordon attended rival high schools in Tulsa, Oklahoma. Even though Gordon was several years older than Amy, they had a great time talking about their hometown and how different it was from Pocatello, and Idaho in general.

It was also fun to watch the subtle flirtations between Amy and Curt. The two shared the back seat of our rusty old Suburban so it was all too easy to eavesdrop on their conversation.

"So, Curt," Amy said, tilting her head ever so slightly. "Are you going to wear your kilt to the game tonight?"

"I don't know. Do you think I should?" he asked, his voice full of sincerity. The guy was quite an actor.

"Sure, why not?" Amy replied. "I admire a guy in touch with his Scottish side."

Curt tapped my shoulder to get my attention. "Hey, Mol. Do we have a Scottish side?"

"I think we have an Irish side. Does that count?" I asked.

Curt turned to Amy. "Does that count?"

"I think some stickler historian or geographer might object, but I think you can take liberties, at least for the game tonight."

"You wouldn't happen to have some green knee socks I could borrow, would you?" Curt asked.

"Awww, man! I left them back at the dorm."

It was at this point that I decided to tune out the two in the seat behind us and tune into Gordon who looked exhausted from juggling a demanding school load as well as two jobs. He reached over and put his arm around me, so I leaned my head onto his shoulder as we drove into the relentless rays of the setting sun.

"Are you going to make it through the football game tonight?" I asked. "You look so tired."

"I'm sure I'll get a second wind when we're there. At least I hope so 'cause I really am beat."

"Do you want me to drive so you can rest a bit?" I asked, but I already knew the answer.

"I'll be fine. Just keep talking to me." Gordon said through a yawn.

It bothered me a bit that Gordon never seemed to be able to step back and let someone else help him out. He truly was a Christlike man in that he always wanted to serve others and be responsible as well, but at times I felt that he overdid it. He wouldn't accept help for almost any reason. I wasn't sure why, either.

"So, how was your day?" I asked.

"Hectic, just like yours." He replied.

"Actually, my day was going great until I ran into Chad Hanks." I straightened out my body and turned on the seat so I was facing Gordon. "Please don't tell me that you and Chad Hanks are some sort of math buddies or something."

Gordon chuckled for a moment but then let out a long sigh. "The guy has always been decent and even quite nice around me, Molly. I've

been tutoring him almost every day for a few weeks now and I haven't
seen this other side of him that you've talked about."

My voice suddenly rose, and I could feel my muscles tense up as I
spoke. "The guy is a total jerk, Gordon. Nothing but a loser. Don't let
his charming ways fool you. He's the guy who got Shannon pregnant
and then abandoned her."

Gordon put his right arm back around my shoulder and pulled me
in closer, probably in an attempt to quiet the storm that was obviously
beginning to rage within me. His voice was calm—too calm—and it
seemed to irritate me even more. "I'm not saying that what the guy
did to your cousin was right. It was awful. Horrible. And I remember
seeing how Shannon struggled last year up at BYU-Idaho as she tried
to fight down the demons from her past. But she was finally able to
move on. Maybe you should too, Molly."

"What?" I nearly shouted as I sat upright again and turned to
face my husband. The playful banter in the back seat suddenly si-
lenced upon my outburst.

Gordon remained calm. "Maybe Chad has repented. Or maybe he
hasn't. We may never know. All I do know is that he seems nice enough
around me, and I can't just suddenly hate the guy for something he
did, what, four . . . five years ago? People can change, Molly."

I couldn't believe what I was hearing. "You're justifying what he
did."

Gordon put his hand on my shoulder. "I'm not. You misunder-
stand, Molly. And I promise you, I'm not justifying his actions. He
was wrong in what he did to Shannon. But don't you think he deserves a chance to redeem himself? Don't you think he's capable of
changing?"

"No!" I replied. "I don't think Chad Hanks is capable of any redeeming qualities."

"Molly . . ." Gordon began to speak, but I cut him off.

"I don't want to talk about this anymore."

Moisture stung my eyes, and my throat ached. Gordon and I had
never argued before. I felt horrible, but why did he have to persist in
defending such a creep.

For the last fifteen minutes of the drive to Oakley, Gordon and I
didn't speak. Curt and Amy eventually resumed their playful banter;
only now it didn't seem quite so cute.

Chapter
EIGHT

It's always an interesting and somewhat unsettling experience to revisit the stomping grounds of your youth. As I sat in the bleachers and looked out onto the Oakley High School football field during the homecoming game, a myriad of images, that I hadn't even realized were still there, began to sweep through my memory as the cool autumn breeze rushed around us.

When I looked off to the left of the field, I couldn't help but notice the short flight of cement steps leading up to the back entrance of the gym. It was the night of the homecoming dance, during my junior year, when I received my first kiss while sitting on those steps. That momentous occurrence in any girl's life was bestowed upon me by the lips of my high school sweetheart, Brandon Mace, who, by the way, wasn't even my date that night.

The football game continued on, but instead of watching my youngest brother, Dusty, as he so diligently attempted to guard the defensive line, I found my eyes scanning the gravel and dirt track that ran the circumference of the football field. A few years back, it was my feet that did the running around this all-to-familiar rural stadium as a member of the track and cross-country teams. The most memorable laps I'd taken at this very location, however, happened on prom night during my junior year. Dressed in complete formal attire, and hand-in-hand, Brandon and I talked about so many different things as we strolled around the perimeter of the field.

"What ya thinking about?" Gordon's voice pierced my thoughts and his touch seemed to reel me back into reality as he gave my knee a playful squeeze.

"Nothing really," I replied, although it wasn't exactly the full truth. It's not like I spend any significant amount of time lost in memories of Brandon Mace. I'd have to blame it on the environment and atmosphere here at the game. The familiarity of it all triggered far-off recollections from my high school days. After my reaction to Chad today, maybe they weren't so far-off after all.

Gordon, always in tune with my psyche, removed his hand from my knee, slid it around my shoulder and pulled me in close. His body was nice and warm and I'd come to depend on that sense of security and peace I felt in his arms.

Gordon leaned over and spoke softly in my ear. "I'm sorry about what happened in the car a bit ago. I didn't mean to upset you."

How did I know that Gordon would be the first to apologize, even though he wasn't the one responsible for my frustration—or outburst.

"It wasn't your fault," I said, and nestled my head onto his shoulder. "I'm sorry I get riled up so easily. I hope you're not going to get tired of me. Eternity is a pretty long time."

Gordon didn't say a word; he didn't need to. He simply snuggled me in even tighter while kissing the top of my head. The two of us sat there perfectly content in our little spot of paradise on the football stadium bleachers, wrapped in Curt's "kilt" while the game raged on.

Halfway through the game Amy, who was sitting on the other side of me—Curt was sitting on the other side of her—leaned over and whispered in my ear.

"Don't look now, but there's this really hot guy over to our right who got here just as the halftime show was starting, and he can't seem to quit staring in our direction."

I started to turn my head to the right but Amy nudged my leg with hers. "Not yet!" She nearly squealed through gritted teeth. "Don't be so obvious."

An uneasy feeling began to settle in my stomach as I speculated who was looking in our direction. Being impatient, however, I scanned the spectators in the bleachers until my eyes fell on that familiar face, which at that very moment was staring right back at me. Brandon—still as handsome as ever—gave me a brief wave and a weak smile and then quickly turned his attentions back to the halftime show.

The whole situation seemed surreal, like an episode out of The Twilight Zone—do-do-do-do, do-do-do-do. Here I was, sitting in the bleachers at my high school football stadium snuggling with my sweetheart—my eternal companion, the love of my life and reason for living (okay, I'll quit)—when I happen to make eye contact with the guy who not too long ago made my heart do flips and my stomach flutter with excitement. The only thing that struck me as amusing with this entire scenario was that my body no longer seemed to give that "Brandon response." And a good thing too, since I was married to someone else. If anything, I felt a little odd and uncomfortable, and I wasn't even sure why.

Having witnessed the brief visual exchange between Brandon and me, Amy leaned over in a subtle manner and whispered in my ear. "I want all the sordid details after the game."

I tilted my head toward my teammate and whispered back into her ear, "I hate to upset you, but there aren't any 'sordid details' to share. We dated a bit in high school and college before I fell madly in love with Gordon."

Amy's expression was dubious. "There's got to be more to the story." She glanced back to Brandon who seemed to be absorbed in the game that had just resumed.

"Nope," I replied. "Sorry."

My friend looked back again at Brandon with narrowed eyes, and then over to Gordon who had his arm around me. He was totally caught up in the game as well. Giving her head a quick tilt over toward Brandon, she said, "He looks scorned, if you ask me."

I couldn't help but laugh at that thought. "What?" Somehow my voice elevated about five octaves, but with the commotion of the game, no one seemed to notice. Everyone was too busy cheering on the team.

"His heart's been broken—I can tell." Amy's voice went melancholy, and if I'd had a violin and knew how to play it, I would have.

"How can you tell?" I asked in disbelief.

"His eyes," She replied, in a rather matter-of-fact tone. "Haven't you ever heard that the eyes are the window to the soul? His soul is hurting, Molly. *He's* hurting, and in a bad way. This boy's having a hard time getting over you."

"So when did you become psychic?" I asked.

Amy nudged me with her shoulder. "I never claimed to be psychic. I'm just good at reading body language and the interactions between people. I tell ya, Molly. The guy's oozing with sorrow. And to see you here with Gordon is just twisting the dagger in his heart."

I couldn't help but roll my eyes with that last statement. "Give me a break. My mom, dad, and even Dusty have all told me that Brandon has taken quite effortlessly to the role of Oakley's most eligible bachelor."

"Well, it's all a show. The guy's broken up inside."

I figured it was no use arguing with Amy about her speculations so I decided to turn my attention to my little brother and his game. After all, that's why I was here, not to revisit the memories of my high school days.

❈❈❈

Our weekend in Oakley was turning into the restful reprieve that most of us needed—at least I did. When I initially woke up Saturday morning, I was a little more tired than usual—go figure! Between basketball practices, late nights with my text books and other stresses related to school, I was stretching the limits of my body's endurance. In an attempt to bring things back into balance, I decided to go back to sleep. My body agreed because the second I closed my eyes, I knew I'd made the right decision. I was asleep again in seconds.

After my much-needed extended sleep, I did do some reading for American Lit while lounging on the couch in the living room. Actually, I started out on an even more comfortable couch in the family room, but Curt and Amy soon invaded my peace and quiet by turning on an ESPN soccer game. Those two had so many similar interests and personality traits that it was a little scary, but it was fun to watch.

Even with all that sleep I'd indulged in earlier, after about an hour of textbook reading, I found my eyelids heavy and I began reading the same line over and over. Deciding to forgo any possibility of ever catching up on my reading assignment at least this weekend, I placed the heavy anthology—still open—on my chest and closed my eyes yet again. I hadn't remembered feeling this exhausted since last winter when I had a nasty bout with the flu. Maybe I had a little bit of a bug. I didn't feel achy or chilled, but I did feel a bit nauseated at times. Whenever I felt like this, it would go away if I ate something. But at the moment, I was just too lazy to get up and get myself something to eat.

Just when I was about to doze off, a fly or dust ball or something began to tickle my nose. Every time I tried to shoo it away, it seemed to come back. After about three attempts with my hand to wave off whatever the culprit was, I opened my eyes to see my goofball husband sitting next to the couch. He wore a mischievous grin on his face and held some sort of feather in his hand.

Before I had any chance to even think about retaliation, Gordon leaned over to place a gentle kiss on my ticklish nose, followed by a second kiss to my lips. How could I shoo that away?

"Hey, Sleeping Beauty, I've come to rescue you," Gordon spoke in a soft voice as he reached up to run his fingers through my hair.

"Rescue me?" I asked.

"Yeah, from this." Gordon lifted my American Lit book off of me and sat it on the coffee table.

I placed my hand to my heart. "My hero."

Gordon picked up my hand and kissed one of my knuckles. "You feeling okay?" He asked.

"I'm fine." I replied.

"Maybe the basketball idea was a little too much on top of all your studies."

"Nah, I'm just being lazy today. And reading this thing," I motioned to my textbook, "doesn't help. I might as well take sleeping pills."

"Well, since you're feeling okay, Curt was talking about going up to City of Rocks for a little climbing adventure. Amy's all psyched about it too. What do you think?"

"Sounds fun," I said, as I attempted to sit up.

❈❈❈

Within the hour, Curt, Amy, Gordon, and I climbed into our rusty old Suburban for the trek up to City of Rocks. Most of the drive was on a dirt road and when we finally arrived, Amy was surprised to see actual rock climbers ascending the vertical granite walls.

"Look at that guy," Amy hollered, pointing to a man who, thank goodness, was secured with harnesses while attempting to ascend somewhat of a ledge three-fourths the way up a particularly intimidating looking cliff. "We're not going to try that, are we?"

"Not today," Curt replied.

"Not in my lifetime," I added. "But we can climb Bathtub Rock. It's been my favorite since I was a little kid."

"Sounds like a good place to start my climbing career," Amy said.

The four of us wandered around the massive boulders, simply absorbing the awe inspiring work of nature before we began our ascent of Bathtub Rock. We didn't talk much on our way up, probably because as amateur climbers, it was important to stay focused on our footing and hand grips.

Since Amy and Curt were ahead of me and Gordon, I couldn't help but notice how attentive my younger brother was to Amy; offering her a helping hand or securing her foothold when necessary. There was definitely something brewing between them, and even though Amy wasn't LDS and Curt was planning on serving a mission at the end of the school year, I wasn't too worried about what I saw developing. Things would work themselves out.

"Whoa! The view is beautiful up here," Amy said as she blocked the sun's glare with her hand while scanning the horizon.

"Yes, it is," Curt replied with his eyes fixed on my very attractive friend. Obviously the kid didn't realize how transparent he was. Gordon and I exchanged knowing glances, but Amy seemed oblivious. Knowing my brother, I was fairly certain she'd figure him out before long.

"Why do they call this Bathtub Rock?" Gordon asked.

"Because of this little pool over here," I replied. "When it rains, it fills with water, like a bathtub."

"Ahhhhh," Gordon said, seemingly pleased with this new bit of trivia. Gordon was a collector of trivia—an unusual hobby.

Amy found a spot to sit and look out onto the surrounding vista and the rest of us followed suit. For a while we all sat in silence as we examined the Lord's creations.

It was Curt who finally broke the tranquility. "I'm really going to miss this place when I'm gone."

"Where are you going?" Amy asked.

"I don't know," Curt replied, " not yet."

Amy looked puzzled. "What do you mean?"

"I'll be going on a mission for my church when school gets out for the summer." Curt continued to look out at the vista as he spoke— almost as if in a trance.

"But you'll be back when school starts again, right?"

"It's a two-year mission," Gordon clarified. "I went on one myself to California—best two years of my life."

I wasn't quite sure if Amy looked a little shocked, or unbelieving, or what. "Wow. So do you make much money doing this mission thing?"

Curt stepped back in the conversation. "Missionaries don't earn money while they're serving out in the field. As a matter of fact, most of us have been saving up for this experience since we were little kids. I've got enough money saved to cover my entire two years."

It was good to hear Curt talk about his mission like this, especially since the past year had been pretty tough on him. Most of us—except for maybe Mom—had been wondering if he was still planning to serve.

Amy seemed a bit shocked by the entire concept. "Wow. Two years? That's such a long time."

"Yeah, especially when you can't date," I teased. Gordon elbowed me, and I wasn't sure why. I was just trying to have a little fun.

"Hey, thanks for reminding me," said Curt.

Now Amy dove back into the conversation. "You mean to tell me that you pay for this mission yourself, and then they tell you that you can't go out on a date for two whole years. Nothing against your religion—I actually respect you for having one. But doesn't this no-dating rule seem a bit extreme?"

Gordon, once again, added the voice of wisdom and reason to our conversation. "When I served in Sacramento, I found it easier to concentrate on my goals as a missionary since I wasn't focusing my attention on dating and girls—which, trust me, can be a huge distraction to nineteen and twenty-year-old guys. Dedicating those two years to serving the Lord and the people of Northern California helped me to become a stronger person physically, emotionally, and mentally. And look here," Gordon put his arm around me. "Things in the 'female' department worked out quite nice for me when my mission was done, wouldn't you say?"

All Amy could do was sigh. And from the sound of it, it didn't sound like a convinced sigh—perhaps even a bit frustrated. Curt, however, still seemed lost in his own thoughts.

Once again, it occurred to me that something was developing here between Curt and Amy. All along, I had encouraged their friendship because the two were alike in so many ways. They seemed like such a good match. But now I was wondering if maybe I'd made a mistake. As much as I'd grown to love Amy, the last thing I wanted was for Curt to start having second thoughts about serving a mission.

Chapter
NINE

The ringing of our telephone jarred my unconsciousness, pulling me back into reality. Apparently, I'd managed to fall asleep sometime after eating lunch—good ol' PB&J. I'd always liked them, but lately I'd even been craving them.

Standing up abruptly to answer the phone sent my head into a spin. I had to steady myself before I could make it across our little living room to reach the cordless that was sitting on the table.

The answering machine had no patience for dizzy spells and began playing its recorded message. *You've reached Gordon and Molly's place. Oh, yeah, and Curt's too. We can't come to the phone right now, but . . ."*

"Hello, hello," I said into the receiver after I was finally able to reach the phone and then turn off the machine.

"Molly?"

Just hearing my cousin Shannon's voice sent a wave of elation through my tired body. The two of us had been best friends our entire lives. Last year we were even roommates up at BYU-Idaho. Now that we were both married and living a good hour and a half away from each other, both of us were suffering with severe withdrawal symptoms from being apart. It was tough!

"Hey there, cuz, what's going on?" I asked.

"Are you sitting down?" Now this statement often precedes bad news, but knowing Shannon as well as I do, I could sense excitement—the happy kind—in the tone of her voice.

I quickly pulled out a chair from the table and took a seat. After my dizzy spell only seconds earlier, I certainly didn't want to take any chances.

"Okay, I'm sitting." I said. "Now tell me, what's going on?"

"Just now, just two minutes ago, I took one of those home pregnancy tests and, well, I'm pregnant."

"No way. Really?"

"Positively!" Shannon squealed. "I'm holding this little pregnancy test, stick-thingy right here in my hand and there's a pink line where it says 'pregnant.'"

"Shannon, this is so awesome! Does Justin know?"

"Not yet. And after his classes he has to work. I'm not going to see him for probably eight more hours and I knew if I didn't tell someone I was going to explode." Shannon almost sounded out of breath.

"Well, I'm glad you called me, but I think *you're* the one who'd better sit down. You're going to pass out from all this excitement," I said.

"I'm fine."

"Well, just humor me and sit down, will ya?"

"I'm sitting, I'm sitting," Shannon said, her voice still full of excitement.

"So, how are you feeling?" I asked.

"I feel incredible—well, tired too but totally incredible."

"I'm so happy for you."

There was a slight moment of silence before Shannon responded. "Molly, I hate to admit this—and I probably wouldn't if I was talking to anybody else. But ever since I gave my little girl up for adoption back in high school, I've had this crazy, awful fear that maybe I'd never get a second chance, you know, at motherhood." Shannon's voice became soft—an extreme change from only moments earlier—and I could tell she was struggling to keep her emotions in check. "I've worried that maybe Heavenly Father wouldn't want to, you know, give me a second chance."

I wanted to say, *That's silly! Heavenly Father doesn't work like that.* But who was I to make light of my cousin's fears and insecurities. After all, I had plenty of my own. Instead, I opted for another route.

"Well, I guess you were wrong." A smile spread across my face as I spoke and I hoped Shannon could hear it in my voice. "Ya know, sometimes it's good to be wrong. And I betcha that before you turn forty, you and Justin'll have a dozen little Collins kids tearing through your house."

It worked. I could hear Shannon chuckling on the other end. "I'm not sure about a dozen, but Justin and I talk about having a large family, just like you and Gordon do, I'm sure."

"Gordon?" I tried to make my voice sound puzzled. "I'm not sure who you're talking about. I live a rather solitary life—well, unless you count Curt. I don't. Oh, but there *is* a guy who crawls into bed with me sometime after midnight every night—kinda cute too—but we never get a chance to talk since I have classes early in the morning."

"I rest my case." Shannon said with a laugh.

"Yeah, well," I could feel my cheeks getting warm and was more than ready to change the subject.

"How are your classes going?" I asked.

"They're fine. How about yours? Do you like ISU?"

"Well, it's a *lot* different from BYU-Idaho. *Totally* different atmosphere, but I'm getting used to it. And I have some pretty nice professors."

"That's good." Shannon's voice suddenly took on a hesitant tone. "Hey, I was wondering, you know, if you ever run into, run into Chad. Chad Hanks."

"Well, as a matter of fact, yeah. And you're not gonna believe this one. Gordon is his math tutor."

"Really?" Shannon seemed amazed at this coincidence as well.

"Yup. And he's still a big jerk."

"Did you talk to him?" Shannon asked.

"Not really." I replied. "I could hardly stand to be in the same room with the guy."

Shannon was very quiet on the other side of the line so I figured I'd better shut up as well. "Well, I'd better go now. I have another class in a little bit and then basketball practice this afternoon."

"I think it's so cool you're playing basketball again, Molly. You're such a natural."

"Yeah, right," I replied. "I'm feeling more like an old lady these days with these sore and stiff muscles. And I'm so tired all the time."

"Well, don't over do it," Shannon warned.

"Yeah, tell that to the coach," I said with a chuckle. "And look who's talking, Little Mommy. You're the one who'd better be taking it easy."

"I will," Shannon promised. "I will."

When Shannon and I hung up, I plopped back down on the couch and kicked my feet up onto the coffee table. *Why was I so dang tired? Was I that out of shape?*

As I gazed out at my pink-painted toenails, I couldn't help but think about Shannon being pregnant. I wondered if it would be a girl. Having a girl would be fun because you could dress her up in little dresses, put ribbons in her hair, and paint her fingernails and toenails. I hoped she was having another girl!

As my line of vision traveled from my pink toenails up my legs and landed on my flat stomach, I wondered what it would feel like to have a belly full of baby. In a sudden spurt of spontaneity, I grabbed the plaid blanket from the couch and rolled it into a ball, shoving it under my navy blue T-shirt. Then I tried to smooth out any lumps; a lumpy pregnant belly would never do. As I looked down at my "creation" I was astonished. Wow! It was hard to imagine that my stomach would ever get this big some day.

I decided I needed a better view, so I got up and headed into the bathroom to check out my new look in the large mirror that extended down to the sink. As I stepped back and then turned my body from side to side with my mass of rolled-up blanket extending, and looking quite convincing, I was half astonished, half amused, and figured that I looked about nine months pregnant—with twins.

Then I placed my hands around the largest part of the "bulge," but instead of looking in the mirror, I looked down. My belly was so round. It almost looked like I had a basketball under my T-shirt.

It was at that very moment that a strange thought occurred to me. Would I rather be embracing pregnancy right now, or would I rather be an Idaho State University women's basketball star? It made me really think about which was more important to me? To be honest, I wasn't sure.

I loved the game of basketball. Over the past couple of years I'd forgotten how much I enjoyed the game until I tried out and made the team here at ISU. I'd forgotten how much I thrived on the competition, the exhilaration, the praise. It felt good to be accomplished in something, and to be recognized for my skills.

Then I thought about motherhood—my own mother in particular. She was certainly an 'accomplished' woman, but was she ever praised for the many things she did for me and my brothers? Well, we did make her breakfast in bed every Mother's Day that I could remember. And I've always complemented her on her excellent cooking skills (or at least I'd done this lately whenever we visited). I guess the old saying is true—*You don't appreciate what you've got until it's gone.*

This definitely applied to Mom's cooking.

"Anyone home?" Curt's deep voice echoed from the living room, and I quickly 'delivered' the plaid blanket from under my shirt just as my brother rounded the corner from the hallway.

"Oh, there you are," he said, looking first at my face and then at the blanket in my hands. "You planning on wearing my kilt somewhere?"

"No!" I replied, perhaps a bit too defensively.

"Good, 'cause I have a *hot* date tonight." Curt had a twinkle in his eyes as he playfully raised his eyebrows up and down. The kid was nothing but a shameless tease! "And knowing how the ladies like my legs and all, I thought I'd go for the Scottish look." Then with a straight face he asked. "Do you think it makes me look like Mel Gibson?"

I threw the blanket over my brother's head. "I think it makes you look like a fool. But I'm just your sister. What do I know?"

Curt pulled the blanket from off his head. "*Amy* likes my blanket."

"Yeah," I replied, "When she's trying to stay warm while sitting next to you at a football game."

"Molly, Molly, Molly. You underestimate the effect I have on women."

How could I argue with that? Curt was right. Females—all females—of any age, seemed to absolutely love my little brother. He had a certain charisma that somehow managed to draw them in. Simply put, the kid was charming. Even to me, his ornery sister. Well, most of the time.

"So do you and Amy have a date tonight?" I asked.

"Actually, I'm going to pick her up after basketball practice. We're going to Taco Bell and then on to the library to study."

"You really like her, don't you?"

"Of course," Curt replied. "What's not to like?"

"Nothing. Absolutely nothing." I wanted to warn him to not lose sight of his mission goals, but was he really serious enough about Amy to warrant such a comment? I doubted it. And knowing my little brother, the last thing I wanted to do was make him feel defensive. He was just being a typical eighteen-year-old, enjoying the dating life. What did I know anyway?

Chapter
TEN

I'm not sure what initially raised the little red flag in my mind—the one that was presently beating me over the head, demanding immediate attention. Perhaps it was the conversation I'd had with Shannon the previous day. Maybe it was the subtle hints from my body—constant fatigue, a slight sense of nausea that would only go away when I ate. Then there was that little dizzy spell and those crazy cravings for peanut butter and jelly. There was only one logical conclusion.

I must be pregnant!

The thought simultaneously sent a wave of excitement and chill of horror through my entire body. Could it possibly be true? And why had I finally figured this out now?

Of course, there was that obvious indication—a missed menstrual cycle. But things in the "girl's department" have never really fit me like your average female. When I was in high school, one doctor indicated my irregular menstrual cycles were due to my heavy involvement in athletics; I went from one sport to the next with the changing seasons like a five-year-old on Halloween, racing from house to house, with no inclination to slow down. Since I was back into basketball full-force, I'd figured that this was why I was running late. Well, one thing was for sure. I needed to find out what was going on—and soon.

In our phone conversation, Shannon mentioned that she'd taken a home pregnancy test to verify she was a mommy-to-be. I wondered if this should be my first step as well. How complicated could it be, anyway? My cousin wasn't a rocket scientist and she figured it out.

I'd never been in the market for one of these pregnancy tests, but I had a notion that the drug store would surely be my best bet. Within eleven minutes, I found myself standing outside of Rite Aid. I was both nervous and anxious.

After making my way across the parking lot and through the electronic doors, I headed straight to the pharmacy section. I was on a mission, and nothing short of an earthquake, or equally devastating natural disaster, would hinder my quest.

Now usually when I'm having trouble locating a particular item in any given store, I have no qualms about seeking assistance from a store employee. But this was different. This was highly personal. This was a test requiring a sample of my bodily fluids, for crying out loud. How could I possibly ask for assistance? I'd rather ask for a bottle of ipecac syrup and down it on the spot than ask for help locating a pregnancy test kit, especially from the pharmacist, Mr. Eyebrows, standing behind his tall counter.

He'd probably laugh at me—a mad scientist kind of laugh to match his unruly eyebrows—and send me off to the candy aisle with a warning that I was too young to be looking for such an item. How could I help the fact that without wearing a generous amount of makeup I happen to look like a fourteen-year-old?

After scanning a half dozen different aisles, a few dozen different times, as well as picking up a bottle of Tums, (I wasn't sure why, other than Shannon said she lived on the things when she'd been pregnant before) I finally came to the conclusion that Rite Aid not only had the most complete selection of feminine hygiene products I'd ever noticed in any given store in the entire state of Idaho, but they obviously didn't sell pregnancy test kits because they were nowhere to be found. Either that or I was blind, out of my mind, or both!

"Can I help you find something?" A female voice broke into the internal frenzy taking place in my head. What kind of loaded question was that anyway? Did I look lost? The truth of the matter was that I was about to lose my mind if I didn't find a darn pregnancy test, and soon.

I turned to see a lady, who was probably old enough to be my mother, wearing a red vest and a friendly smile. She looked harmless enough if I could just move past my reservations, and embarrassment, and ask her the simple question. Finally, my desperation prevailed.

"Yeah, um, could you tell me where the, you know," I lowered my voice and leaned in close so she could hear, "where, um, the pregnancy tests are?"

I might as well have asked for a pair of toenail clippers or a bottle of Pepto Bismol. The lady was totally unfazed by the nature of the item I'd requested, thank goodness.

They were situated in a locked glass cabinet between some items to help with the effort to quit smoking and kits that I gathered help you to know when you're fertile. It was all very confusing, and the lady in the red vest seemed to be hovering over me. I wanted to ask for her recommendation but since she looked about as old as my mom I figured she was well beyond this phase of her life.

I finally settled on a twin pack, two kits in one—at least that's what I thought it meant—and headed for the checkout. After glancing at my watch, I realized that I'd been in the store for forty-five minutes. All I had to do now was pay for this thing (as well as the Tums) and make a mad dash for my truck. I'd have my answer in a matter of minutes.

Unfortunately, of the numerous check out stations at the front of the store, only one was open. Why do these places bother to construct several check outs when they are *never* open?

After standing in line for what seemed ten years behind a lady who was purchasing a cart-full of miscellaneous items ranging from silk floral decorations to a silver toe ring that needed a price check, I finally made it to the front of the line. I was ready to make my purchase and get out of this place.

The girl at the register looked quite young (as opposed to the lady who had unlocked the cabinet for me) and seemed friendly and conscientious in her work.

"Did you find everything you were looking for?" She asked.

"Yep." I replied, though I wasn't really in the mood for small talk.

The girl scanned in the Tums and the register made its little beep. Then she picked up the pregnancy test kit, holding it much too high so that the elderly man in line behind me buying Polident, and the lady juggling a newborn behind him could see.

"Did you know that the store brand pregnancy tests are on sale this week?"

"That's okay. I'll just get this one," I said in a hushed and hurried voice. Then, for some reason, perhaps to justify my choice, I added. "I need two, anyway."

Before the checkout lady had another chance to question my purchases, I placed a crisp twenty in front of her and then glanced apologetically at those behind me.

When the purchase was finally complete, I snatched my bag and headed for the parking lot. Only twenty more yards to the truck and I'd be free and clear and one step closer to knowing if I was indeed pregnant.

"Molly!"

The female voice calling my name was quite familiar—all the more reason to pretend I didn't hear it and flee the scene. But I did hear it. Since I'm an awful liar, I knew I needed to turn to the voice—Janice Judd, the Relief Society President of our married student ward—and try not to look like I was about to find out some life-altering news (if I could ever make it to my truck and back to The Cave so I could take the test).

I turned and waved to my approaching Relief Society president with my free hand while maneuvering the bag to where it was almost hiding behind my leg.

Janice's husband was working on a master's degree, and they had been at this married student gig for quite some time. She had their three little ones in tow—a preschooler, a toddler, and a newborn—and she looked, well, tired.

"Hey, Molly, how's the basketball going?" she asked, but then the toddler broke free from her grasp and started heading back out into the busy parking lot. "Jordan Paul," she hollered as she dashed toward the little fellow whose stout legs were surprisingly quick. "You get back here right now!"

I was impressed how Janice was able to snatch his pudgy, flailing arm with one hand while securing her newborn's head—who was strapped to her front side in a baby carrier—with the other. The preschooler, a little girl, continued to stand next to me, thank goodness. It made me wonder how mothers were supposed to handle numerous children when they themselves had only two hands. I wasn't sure if I was awed or terrified.

"That was a no-no," Janice said in a stern voice to the little guy who, actually, looked quite pleased with himself. Then she turned her attention to me. "Sorry about that. Jordan is our little Houdini— escaping from everything. I think I'm going to have to resort to a leash, for his own safety." Janice laughed, so I did too, though I found little humor in her words. What the heck had I gotten myself into? Now I was wondering if I really did want to go home and take this test. Was I really up for motherhood?

The well-behaved girl started tugging on a strap of the baby carrier that was hanging down. "Mommy, I gotta go potty."

"Please don't pull on that, Maddie."

"But I gotta go." The little girl squealed as she crossed her legs.

"Hey, you look busy," I commented as I casually crossed my own legs, realizing that Maddie and I had something more in common than our somewhat rambunctious younger brothers. "I'd better let you get her to the bathroom."

Janice sighed. "Well, it was good to see you."

"Yeah, you too," I replied, relieved that I could finally head for home.

"Oh, Molly?" Janice hollered since we were now a good ten yards away.

I turned yet again toward her voice.

"You'll let me know if there is anything I can do for you, right?" said the woman with rings under her eyes and three young children connected to her. Now, I've learned throughout the years that this particular statement is often flung around in typical Mormon conversation—especially by home and visiting teachers. But the minute Janice said the words I knew that they came from her heart. She was sincere, and I was humbled. I realized that if I was ever going to make it at this motherhood thing, I was going to have to take the focus off of myself and turn it toward others.

In response, I simply smiled, waved back to Janice and then headed for the truck. Ready or not, I needed to find out if motherhood was soon to come.

❈❈❈

As I sat in the most obvious seat in the bathroom, closed my eyes, and started counting to sixty—after all, the instructions said that I could read the test results in as little as one minute—I found myself praying instead of counting.

Heavenly Father, I'm not even sure I'm ready to see the answer to this pregnancy test, but if you think I'm ready for this step in my life, then I can accept that. But I'm definitely going to need your help! I mean, what if I'm a heavy sleeper and don't hear my baby's cries? What if I never figure out how to nurse a baby and it practically starves? What if I just can't handle changing a diaper with all that stink involved? What if I don't notice when my toddler runs out into a busy parking lot so I have to put him on a leash and people think I'm nuts? What if for the rest of my life I have to walk around with rings under my eyes? What if I just can't do it, Heavenly Father?

In my feeble attempt to seek guidance from above, I found myself reciting a list of my fears and churning up every insecurity I've ever had in my life—not a great place for me to dwell.

At that moment, however, I realized that more than sixty seconds had passed. My eyes flew open and I looked to the edge of the bathtub where the narrow testing stick sat. And there, in the little circle marked "pregnant," was a straight, pink line.

The heaviness in my heart was instantly replaced with nothing less than pure joy. My fears were eased with a sense of purpose, commitment, and gratitude. So what if I had no clue about the particulars of what was about to transpire in my life. One thing, however, was certain.

I was pregnant!

I was going to be a mother!

Chapter
ELEVEN

Hey, what's with the jeans?" Amy asked as I entered the gym. Usually at this time, I'd be wearing athletic shorts, a T-shirt, and my Nike tennis shoes, but I was still in the clothes I'd worn to school that day—and still in a bit of shock with the news I had received minutes earlier.

Only two other team members were out on the court warming up, and the coach hadn't even arrived yet. I figured this was as good a time as any to let my friend in on my little secret.

Under different circumstances, I would have preferred to share this news with Gordon first. But my reality, however, was that basketball practice was about to start. I couldn't just *not* show up—that wasn't my style. Before I talked to the coach, however, there was someone else I wanted to tell.

"Come on over here." I motioned Amy to the bleachers with my head.

"What's up?" my friend asked, a look of concern suddenly altering her usual carefree expression.

"You want the good news or the bad news?" I asked.

"Does the bad news have anything to do with Curt?"

"Nope." I replied, and sensed a slight hint of relief in my friend's expression.

"Okay. Go for the bad news. I'll try to be strong." Amy squinted her eyes shut as if my words might inflict some sort of cruel and unusual punishment to her psyche.

"I'm quitting the team—today."

Amy's eyes suddenly opened wide, along with her mouth. It took a few seconds, however, before she could find any words.

"No way," Amy said. But when I gave a slight nod and shrugged my shoulders, she quickly clasped her hands in front of her as if in prayer and took on a pleading expression. "Please, oh please, oh please tell me you're kidding."

When I didn't respond, she continued on. "You can't do this to me, Molly." Now she was clutching my arm with her hands. "You're my lifeline on this team. I won't survive without you."

I was touched by the sincerity of Amy's expression and words, but still, it didn't change the fact that I was pregnant.

"Maybe I should tell you the good news to help you understand."

"And that would be . . . ?" Amy raised an eyebrow as if nothing I could say would help her accept my decision.

"Well, you're not going to believe this, but I'm pregnant."

"No! Really? You're sure?" It looked like a battle was taking place with Amy's emotions.

"I just took the test less than an hour ago. I doubt it was defective."

"So, how do you feel? Are you're happy about this? Are you ready to have a baby?"

"Happy? Yes, I think." I took a deep breath. "Yes, definitely!"

Amy folded her arms in front of her. "You sound like you're trying to convince yourself."

"I'm not. Really! It's just the 'ready' part of your question that concerns me. I'm not sure what that's supposed to mean. How does someone *ever* know when they're ready for parenthood? It's not like you can practice. When it happens it's like 'ready or not.' It's not like you have a choice in the matter."

"Well, there's *always* a choice," Amy said with a wave of her hand. Her words, though spoken in a carefree manner, felt like a punch to my stomach.

"What do you mean? Like abortion?" I somehow managed to ask.

Amy's expression quickly softened. She must have realized that the two of us were on totally different wavelengths on this issue. "Look, I'm sorry, Molly. I have no business even bringing up a subject like this. It really wasn't my intention to ruin the moment for you. Of course you're happy and ready." Amy put her arm around my shoulder. "You and Gordon are going to make great parents. But it still stinks in a big way that you're leaving the team. I'm just selfish and want you to stay to keep me sane."

I was touched by Amy's concern for my well being but also stunned by her statement about "choice," referring to the legal choice to have an abortion. I thought I knew my friend well. Our personalities were alike in many ways, but this was a subject that we obviously didn't share the same views on.

This realization was quite upsetting, but then I had to reflect on my friend's background. She wasn't raised like I was in a home with a religious foundation. We didn't have the same understanding, and I couldn't hold that against her. I could only love her as a friend and hopefully be an example to her of the positive values I was raised with. And when all was said and done, nothing changed the fact that Amy was a wonderful person and friend. What more could I ask for?

As we sat on the bleachers talking, Coach Hill entered the gym. The sense of dread I felt was suddenly oppressive. I was *not* looking forward to the conversation that was about to take place, but it was inevitable.

"Here comes the big guy," said Amy. "You want me to hold your hand while you do this?"

"I'll be fine—I think," I replied and stood (ready or not) to inform the coach that I was about to mess up his carefully constructed roster—and my newfound dream to play college basketball.

※※※

When I pulled the truck up in front of the grocery store it was 9:50 P.M. and Albertsons would be closing in ten more minutes. I didn't have much time to spare, so I hurried inside.

At exactly 10 P.M. I looked at my watch then picked up a little jar of creamed spinach. How babies could choke this stuff down was beyond me. I replaced the green jar and scanned the other selections—none of which looked appetizing (well, except for something called Hawaiian Delight. At least someone in the baby food industry decided to take pity on the little guys and their developing taste buds).

I looked back at my watch again—10:01. Maybe my watch was running fast. I was about to turn my attention to the selection of teething biscuits on the top shelf when the voice that I'd been waiting for—the night manager, Dave—came over the store intercom.

"Attention Albertsons Shoppers. The time is now 10 P.M. and our store is closed. Please take your purchases to a checkout counter and thank you for shopping at Albertsons. Oh, and will Albertsons associate Gordon Nelson please report to aisle nine for customer assistance."

My heart suddenly leapt as I realized that my plan was now in motion (with a little help from some of Gordon's co-workers). I looked down at both ends of the aisle not knowing for sure which direction my husband would be coming from.

I was the only one in the entire aisle, and I was glad for that. It would make the moment all the more special. I wandered down a few steps to check out the vast diaper selection. Did it really matter what brand you used? There was a significant price difference and, no doubt, Gordon and I would opt for the least expensive brand—unless they totally didn't work.

"Hey," came that familiar voice from behind me. "What are you doing here?"

"Just checking up on you," I said. "How's your shift going?" I asked, not that I expected some detailed or interesting response. I was simply stalling. I was nervous.

"Oh, you know, you've seen one box of Lucky Charms, you've seen 'em all."

"Yeah, I suppose."

"Hey," my husband said, looking a bit distracted. "Have you seen anyone else on this aisle in the last minute or so?" Now it was Gordon who was looking up and down the baby paraphernalia aisle.

"Nope. I've been the only one standing here for the past five minutes or so."

Gordon scratched the back of his head for a good ten seconds before his body suddenly froze—elbow extended and fingers lodged in his thick mane of sandy blond hair. Then slowly, my husband lowered his arm and looked into my eyes.

"Molly?"

"Yeah."

"Why are you standing in the middle of the baby aisle here at Albertsons at ten o'clock at night," Gordon's eyes briefly shifted to the merchandise on the shelves but then quickly returned, "looking at diapers?"

Only two minutes earlier I had known every single word that I'd wanted to say at this very moment. I'd been rehearsing them since I saw that little pink line in the pregnancy test indicating a positive result a few hours ago. But now that I was looking into the clear blue eyes of Gordon—the man who somehow managed to make me love him more and more with each passing second—I could hardly remember my middle name let alone my rehearsed speech. The only function of my body that seemed to be working at the moment was my smile, and it was running on overdrive.

My husband's eyes somehow seemed to be absorbing the situation and were growing larger by every enlightening moment.

As Gordon slowly approached me, his eyes briefly shifted to my stomach but quickly returned to my face.

"You aren't . . ." There was an awkward pause. "You're not . . ."

I simply shrugged my shoulders.

"You are?" Gordon's eyebrows raised along with the tone of his voice.

"Yep." I finally found my voice.

"You mean," Gordon reached out and grabbed a pack of Huggies with a bald baby printed on the packaging, jabbing his index finger into the face of the cute little tyke. "we're going to have one of these?"

"A baby. In May."

Gordon's face was now beaming, but he also looked disbelieving. "No. Really?"

"Really."

Without another word, and in one swift move, my husband dropped the bag of diapers, pulled me into his arms and spun me around right there in the aisle of Albertson's.

A great round of applause sounded from both ends of the baby aisle as Gordon's coworkers—and my conspirators—cheered us on.

And then, with a flair of dramatics, Gordon leaned me back in a low dip like we used to perform in our ballroom dance routine. The finishing touch came with a sweet and gentle kiss placed delicately on my lips.

Gordon Nelson—the father of my children. He sure knew how to take my breath away!

Chapter
TWELVE

It didn't take long for word to spread that I was in the family way. As a matter of fact, when Amy met up with Curt after basketball practice—an everincreasing occurrence lately—she revealed my secret. The two headed for the T-shirt shop in the mall where they had a maternity shirt customized for me with the words "Half Nelson" inscribed across the belly. (Did I mention that Curt had been a high school wrestler?) When they gave it to me, I wanted to explain that there was a *whole* Nelson growing within me, but what more could I expect from the two sports enthusiasts in my life?

I called Mom the morning after I told Gordon about the pregnancy, and she seemed to take the news well—I think.

"Oh, Molly," Mom's voice began to quiver even before she got to the second syllable of my name. "I'm so happy for you."

Now, Mom was already a grandma (twice over), but I guess this time was a bit different for her since I'm her only daughter.

"I'm happy too," I replied.

"Have you seen a doctor yet?"

Why wasn't I surprised that this would be one of the first comments regarding my pregnancy that would pass from my mother's lips? Perhaps because the woman always has been, and always will be, somewhat neurotic (and I mean this in the most loving form of the word) when it comes to the well-being of her offspring.

While growing up, whenever I had even the slightest hint of a cold, Mom would start in with her Vitamin C and chicken soup therapy. If I wasn't sucking on one of those little orange-flavored vitamins, I'd be sipping chicken broth or hot lemon juice that was sweetened with a touch of honey. Mom had a home remedy for everything, and they usually worked.

When Mom mentioned the word doctor, a rather uneasy feeling settled deep within my already nauseous stomach.

"So when am I supposed to see a doctor?" I almost hated to ask.

"As soon as possible."

I let out a deep sigh, and Mom instantly knew what I was thinking—she'd always been kind of scary that way.

"I realize how much you dislike the doctor's office, but . . ."

I cut her off mid-sentence. "Mom, I dislike eating beets. I dislike the color purple—at least on me. And I really dislike having the eight-thirty church schedule every third year. But if we're talking doctors, the word 'dislike' simply isn't adequate. Let me put it this way: I'd almost rather give up electricity, fudge-covered Oreos, and the right to vote in order to avoid this whole prenatal exam issue. That's how serious this is, Mom! Maybe I should have been a pioneer woman. 'Let's pull the wagon over, honey, and let the others pass while I hop in the back; I think little Hyrum or Eliza is ready to arrive.'"

"Where in the world do you get these ideas?" Mom sounded like she was trying to stifle a laugh, and I could just envision her shaking her head back and forth as we spoke. "And trust me, you *wouldn't* want to deliver a baby in the back of a covered wagon. You know, Molly, these pregnancy examinations may not be the most comfortable experience for a woman, but they really are necessary."

"Yeah." I could feel my rebellious side taking over. "Well, the pioneer women didn't have them."

"The pioneer women were probably attended by midwives." Mom seemed to know everything.

"Then I want a midwife, too." I'm afraid I sounded a bit like a two-year-old demanding a cookie. But to be honest, I was simply afraid—mostly of the unknown.

"There are midwives around, honey. And there are wonderful obstetricians. Why don't you ask for recommendations from the gals in your ward? I'm sure you'll get some good referrals." *Mom—always the voice of reason.*

"Yeah, I suppose," I replied. "There's always 'doctor talk' going on in the hall between meetings at church. Either that, or they're swapping tactics on how to get kids to sleep through the night—not one of my problems, yet."

Mom could obviously sense my discomfort over this whole prenatal issue and was trying her best to settle my nerves. "I believe there are even certified nurse midwives that can deliver babies in hospitals."

"Really?"

"We'll have to look into it, but I'm sure we can find someone you'll feel comfortable with for these prenatal visits."

I wasn't sure if I totally believed this, but what could I do about it now. I was pregnant—really and truly, one hundred percent, bun-in-the-oven pregnant. Regardless of Amy's comment the previous day, for me there was no backing out. It simply wasn't an option. Not even a consideration. This gift of giving life was far too precious to me.

So maybe I'd have to be poked and prodded a bit for the next eight months. I may not like it—actually, I'd hate it—but I knew I could handle the situation (as long as I didn't think about it too much). And in the end, I'd be the one walking away with the grand prize—our newborn baby. A *whole* Nelson.

※ ※ ※

Discovering that I was pregnant was very similar to the child-hood experience of returning home on Halloween night with a huge bag of candy. I'd fulfilled one of my greatest desires—to become pregnant—and the initial taste was certainly sweet. But it didn't take long for other by-products of my "fruitful" evening to creep in—most notably, nausea. (And weight gain was sure to follow. Ugh).

On Saturday morning, as I sat on the couch next to my brother Curt, who seemed to be entranced in some absurd cartoon while munching on a plate full of Pop Tarts, I felt as if my body was inca-pable of doing anything short of wallowing in its miserable state of nauseousness. An empty mixing bowl was secured under my chin—for safety purposes—by a stack of three pillows on my lap. My only desire, at the moment, was to rid my stomach of its turmoil through natural means—throwing up. Either that, or instantaneous death (which at the moment didn't seem like such an awful idea).

Fortunately for me—unfortunately for my brother—the prior oc-curred rather abruptly—and it wasn't pretty. Curt, abandoning all thoughts of his Pop Tarts, and clutching his own stomach, fled in a mad dash to the bathroom. Considering the fact that the kid could down three chili-cheese dogs and a grotesque amount of sauerkraut in one sitting, his reaction seemed pretty wimpy.

Gordon, hearing the commotion, in a half-conscious state (he'd worked the late shift the previous night), stumbled into the living room to see what was happening.

"You okay, Mol?" I could hear the concern in my husband's voice, but I was still in the purging process and, well, aside from the fact that I'd always been taught not to speak with my mouth full, I simply couldn't respond.

After a minute or so, when I'd completed my business, I looked up with watery eyes and slack jaw into Gordon's face, which was now rather pale.

"Do I look okay?"

I didn't *mean* to snap at my husband. I didn't *want* to snap at my husband. But I did.

Thank goodness, Gordon didn't take the bait. He simply walked over to the kitchen, ripped off a few paper towels, and brought them to me so I could wipe off my mouth.

"Can I take this?" He asked in reference to the half-full bowl clutched in my hands rather than my foul mood.

I nodded, since at the moment, talking seemed too much of an effort.

In a few minutes, Gordon returned to the living room and cracked open the window allowing the brisk fall air to make its way into the room. It must have rained the previous night because the smell of damp earth wafted through the gentle breeze bringing a much-needed freshness to the room and enlivening my senses.

After closing my eyes and taking a few deep breaths, I willed my body to relax as it fell back into the soft cushions of the couch. "I think I'm finally starting to feel better."

Curt rounded the corner as I spoke, still clutching his stomach. "Well, I'm not."

"Hey bro," Gordon said as he walked over and playfully slapped Curt on the back. "I don't think morning sickness is supposed to be contagious."

"Tell that to my stomach."

Gordon laughed. I wanted to as well but could only manage a weak smile and a slight groan.

"I think you two need more fresh air."

On Gordon's advice, Curt walked over to the window, which was fairly high up since we were in a basement apartment, and took a deep breath. "I think you're right."

"What do you say we all get out of The Cave today and have

some fun? We can catch the football game this afternoon." Gordon's eyebrows were raised in anticipation.

My brother, with his nose still pressed to the screen on the window, agreed. "Now we're talking. And with the activity pass on our student ID's, we get in free."

"We like free," I managed to add.

Gordon walked to the couch and sat down next to me, taking my hand in his. "You think you're up to this?"

Now that some fresh air was reaching my pregnant brain cells I could finally appreciate my husband's concern. "Yeah, I think so."

Gordon reached up and ran a finger across my damp forehead, straightening a loose clump of hair that was held together by the moisture. "Good."

"What time does the game start?" Curt asked.

"I think it starts at one—at least that's what Chad told me."

Just the mention of that name brought on a fresh wave of nausea.

"Chad Hanks?" Curt asked, sounding just a little too excited. Of course, Curt was only thinking about the legendary Oakley High School football hero, not the creep who fathered our cousin's baby and then abandoned Shannon and any responsibility he should have taken. And for what? His egotistical pursuit of football glory.

But worst of all, my husband seemed to *enjoy* talking to the guy, and he did it several times a week while tutoring him in math. He even suggested that maybe Chad had changed his ways and deserved the benefit of a second chance. Next thing, he'd probably want to invite him over for dinner. Well, there was no way I'd ever share a pot of spaghetti with that guy. Never!

"Chad was telling me about the game when I was tutoring him yesterday," said Gordon. "It's supposed to be quite a showdown against Sacramento State University. He suggested that we come early to get good seats."

I wondered if I should confess to my husband that I'd rather watch a twenty-four hour "Barney does Broadway" marathon than go out of my way to watch Chad Hanks play two hours of football—or do anything for that matter. I wondered if he was even worried about my feelings on the matter.

Curt's words broke into my thoughts and I was grateful for the diversion. "Hey, do you think Amy would want to come with us?"

"Probably," I replied. "She seems to want to do anything you're involved with these days."

My younger brother looked pleased.

"Ya know, Curt, if we were kids, I'd accuse you of stealing one of my best friends."

"Well, we're not, and I can't seem to help myself." Curt confessed with a wistful smile. "There's just something about that girl. She's so, so…" He couldn't seem to find the right word. I'd never seen my usually confident brother so distracted. "I can't even pinpoint what exactly it is about her."

"It's because she's incredibly wonderful," I replied.

Curt raised his finger up into the air. "Bingo."

"But don't lose sight of what's most important right now."

"Like what?" My brother asked, a hint of challenge in his voice.

"Like the fact that you've decided to serve a mission at the end of the school year."

Curt rolled his eyes. "Please, Molly, don't start pulling a 'Mom and Dad' on me."

"What's that supposed to mean?" Now my hands were on my hips and, no doubt, I was doing a spot-on imitation of our mother. And the scary part: it happened quite naturally, like a reflex, a hiccup, a sneeze. I wondered if the overabundance of "mommy hormones" had anything to do with my present disposition. No doubt, in the future I'd also be compelled to say irritating "mommy" phrases like "just wait till your father gets home," and "what part of 'no' do you *not* understand?" *My poor kids!*

Curt's words broke into my thoughts. "Don't start preaching to me like I'm a little kid, because I'm not."

I was a little taken back by the edge to Curt's tone. Usually the guy was so happy-go-lucky.

Gratefully, Gordon stepped in, giving Curt a playful nudge before picking up a Pop Tart from the ground, taking a huge bite of it, and speaking with his mouth full. "You're *not* a little kid?"

"Hey," Curt protested. "That was my breakfast on the floor. You're eating my breakfast." He seemed to be back to his usual self.

"Finders, keepers," Gordon taunted, popping the remainder of the frosted tart into his mouth. An impromptu wrestling match ensued, and Curt began pulling out all of his high school wrestling moves, including a *real* half nelson.

Poor Gordon—he didn't stand a chance!

Chapter
THIRTEEN

The Holt Arena, an indoor football stadium—also referred to as the Mini-Dome—was packed with thousands of exuberant ISU Bengal football fans. Gordon had managed to get the four of us some pretty good seats, and although I had misgivings about contributing even an ounce of enthusiasm toward a game in which Chad Hanks was participating, I could gradually feel my stubbornness dissipating as my spirits lifted with the excitement of the atmosphere. Maybe I'd taken my grudge too far. Why not have a little school spirit and cheer for my own team? Certainly, I was capable of that.

Gordon and Curt were situated on each end while Amy and I sat next to each other in the stadium seats. I was grateful for this arrangement. I mean, really now, how fun is a football game without a little girl-talk distraction mixed in with the grunting, groaning, and sweating of half-crazed, testosterone-elevated guys—and that doesn't even include the players out on the field. I always knew Curt was a football fanatic, but I was a bit surprised to see my generally calm-as-a-clam husband practically snorting steam whenever a penalty was called on the Bengals. Must be a guy thing!

Another interesting phenomenon occurred while we sat in the huge athletic arena. Pregnant women began to emerge from nowhere and everywhere. Where were they coming from and why hadn't I noticed them before? I was amazed at the number of round tummies bulging forth in one place at one time—well, aside from any given Relief Society function of our married student ward, but that was to be expected.

And then there were the babies. Tons of babies. Screaming, sleeping, drooling, smiling (and most likely smelly) babies. There were babies snuggled up to their parent in carriers and slings "kangaroo-style," and babies nestled in every brand and model of fabric-lined plastic carrier. My initial thought was, *who would bring a baby to a football game?* I soon learned, however, that lots of people do this. And after a minute or two of reflection, I thought, *why not?* We certainly can't expect parents with little ones to hole away for several years until their child's attention span exceeds a half-hour of Blues Clues or they can distinguish each Muppet or Teletubbie by name. If we waited for this, society as we know it would cease to exist.

"Molly?" Amy's elbow made direct contact with my arm. "You didn't answer me."

"I'm sorry. What did you say?"

"Which one's the creep? You know, the guy you hate so much." Amy was flipping through the football program Curt had purchased before the game started. It displayed a picture of each football player along with position, statistics, and brief background information.

I'd said that I hated Chad Hanks and called him a creep at least a hundred and one times over the last few years—if not to myself, to anyone who would listen. But hearing my own words coming from someone else made me realize how derogatory it actually sounded. I made a mental note to express my feelings in a kinder tone when referring to the guy. Perhaps I'd call him "unsavory." Nah, that sounded like I was referring to a tuna casserole gone bad. Maybe I'd label him "diabolical." Actually, that sounded like it belonged to a comic book villain or James Bond's nemesis. Maybe I just needed to keep my thoughts about Chad Hanks' character to myself.

I picked up the program and turned a few pages until I came to that somewhat familiar face, although he looked older now and a good thirty pounds heavier—most of which was probably muscle. He still had the "golden-boy" image with his sun-bleached hair and engaging blue eyes.

"Here he is." I said, pointing to Mr. Beautiful.

Amy leaned in close and spoke in a low voice—probably so the guys wouldn't hear. "Whoa, he sure is a good-looking creep."

"Yeah, well, once you get to know him, it's easy to see beyond the pretty face."

"Very sad." Amy said with an exaggerated sigh.

"What? What's sad?"

"To waste such a gorgeous face on a creep. Are you sure he hasn't reformed?"

"Never!"

"How do you know?"

My friend's question managed to prick a nerve. "Now you're starting to sound like Gordon."

"And that's a bad thing?" Amy raised an eyebrow.

I took a moment to contemplate as I looked over at my red-faced husband who was hollering at the ref—with his mouth full—and pumping a fistful of popcorn in the air. A few kernels escaped between his fingers (at least I prayed they were from his fingers and *not* from his mouth) and landed in the naturally curly hair of the girl seated in front of us. I was grateful she didn't notice and I was even tempted to pick them out, but I resisted. Laughing to myself at the scene playing out in front of me, a new wave of emotion began seeping into my heart. Gordon was a good man—and wise—not to mention a crazy football fan. Maybe I needed to give his assessment of Chad Hanks a second thought. Maybe.

As the game continued on, I noticed two other things. Chad Hanks really *was* a talented athlete. I couldn't tell you the exact name of his position. Perhaps running back or halfback because he was constantly in possession of the ball with it securely nestled under his arm as he darted in and out of mammoth looking guys with only one objective on their mind—to bring number 32, Chad Hanks, down. If it weren't for my allegiance to Idaho State University, I'd be tempted to root for the other team.

Then there was Curt and Amy. They seemed to be enjoying each other's company more and more these days. It was probably halftime when I noticed that the two were holding hands. And while the matchmaker in me was thrilled with this blossoming romance, another side of me was worried. I would hate to see anything distract Curt from serving a mission. From previous conversations I knew that this was a sensitive subject for my brother.

I'd seen firsthand the wonderful growth and benefits that came from serving a mission; first in my older brothers Alex and Blake, and then with Brandon Mace. Trust me; you learn a lot about someone during two years of faithful letter writing, not to mention the dating that took place before and after his missionary service.

I didn't meet Gordon until after he returned from his mission, but as a convert to the Church, he constantly stated that his missionary service was a pivotal point in his life that simply couldn't be replaced.

I can't help but be thankful for the experiences and knowledge he gained during his two years of service. Our family, our children, will always be blessed because of it.

I was startled from my reverie when the crowd seemed to explode in cheers. Everyone around me was suddenly on their feet in near hysteria. The sound was deafening; the atmosphere electrifying.

"Did you see that?" Gordon hollered as he swooped me up into his arms and kissed me firmly on the lips. "Incredible! Simply incredible!"

It would have been nice if he was referring to my kiss, but I wasn't that dense or delusional.

"I missed it. What happened?" I asked.

"The creep made a touchdown." Amy hollered over the buzz.

"Hey, you're talking about my friend there," Gordon said with a slight scowl on his face but with pride radiating through his voice.

"Sorry." Amy shrugged and then motioned toward me as if I'd made her say it. What a friend!

Curt, oblivious to everything but the current celebration, hollered across Amy and me so his voice would reach Gordon's ears.

"We've got this baby bundled up! There's no way Sac State's going to pull ahead now. Physically impossible!"

I had to laugh at Curt's baby reference? Was it subliminal on my brother's part or was I just ultra aware of anything pertaining to the little "diapered ones" these days? Probably both.

Curt was right. In the remaining two minutes, the ball traveled in each direction for several yards, but the score remained the same and the Bengals rejoiced in sweet victory.

Later on that evening, Chad Hanks was interviewed on Channel 6 News, and even though he was dripping with sweat and probably exhausted, that same old charm that was so prevalent back in high school was still evident—the guy was still as suave and polished as ever.

I had to wonder if Shannon was watching up in Rexburg. I was fairly sure they watched the same television stations as Pocatello, but I couldn't bring myself to call. She had obviously moved on in her life. Justin was a great guy that loved her more than she probably even loved herself, and they, too, were expecting their first baby. Who was I to dredge back up the scum from Shannon's past?

There I go again, I thought. Why did I hate this guy so much? At least this time I only thought the malicious things instead of verbalizing them. Progress, right? Okay, a semi-pathetic rationalization but progress nonetheless.

Gordon had the night off—a rare occasion—and Curt and Amy decided to go to the campus movie. They asked us if we wanted to join them, but we only had to exchange glances for one nanosecond to realize that we could have two precious hours of a Saturday night all to ourselves with no little brother to thwart a potentially romantic evening. We graciously declined.

After they left, we decided to splurge on Chinese takeout since we were both hungry and hadn't eaten since the popcorn at the game. While Gordon went to pick up the food, I decided to shower and get spruced up a bit. I wanted to get rid of the lingering smells on my clothes, skin, and hair from the earlier football game.

I was just putting on the finishing touches of mascara when I heard Gordon descending the stairs into the living room. The aroma of the food in little white cartons infused the air, tempting my nose and making my mouth water. Oh, how I loved a good egg roll, some fried rice, and anything sweet and sour.

As I twisted the lid back onto the mascara, Gordon rounded the corner of the bathroom and gave a low whistle as he looked at my reflection in the mirror.

"My goodness, Mrs. Nelson. You sure know how to make a guy weak in the knees."

I wanted to respond but found myself speechless as my husband approached me from behind, rested his chin on my head, and wrapped his arms around my waist.

Now Gordon seemed speechless as he simply stared at my reflection in the mirror, absorbing every angle and line of my face. After a moment I spoke. Not because I felt uncomfortable. On the contrary, I felt like we were sharing just a little moment of heaven.

"Whatcha thinking about?" My voice was soft to match the moment.

"I was just thinking how beautiful you are, and how wonderful it is that my children get to have you for their mother."

It was at that moment that I realized the palms of Gordon's hands were resting on my still perfectly flat stomach that much too often felt nauseated these days, and was sure to expand in the coming months.

"You're not going to think that in seven months when I'll look like I swallowed a basketball."

Gordon kissed the top of my head and gave my stomach a little pat with his fingers. "Actually, I can't wait. I'm going to read to your belly, rub lotion on it, and talk to it every night."

The thought of this brought a smile to my face and an intense surge of love through my heart. I turned around and gave my husband a kiss, one that he surely wouldn't forget any time soon.

When our lips finally parted, Gordon's voice, slightly husky, filled my ears.

"You know what one of the greatest inventions of the twenty-first century is, Molly?"

Gordon's obscure question made me laugh. I'd learned long ago to "go with the flow" of my husband's thought process. As crazy as it may sometimes seem, he always has a valid point to make.

"I dunno," I said with a giggle. "What?"

Gordon's eyes turned playful and slightly mischievous. "The microwave—'cause you can reheat your food when you're ready to eat."

"Well, thank goodness we have a microwave." I replied.

Gordon simply smiled.

Chapter
FOURTEEN

I wasn't quite sure when it happened; it kind of snuck up on me. It must have been sometime around finals. It's hard to say for sure because basically my brain was crammed with more pertinent information related to my upcoming exams—information that would no doubt leave as quickly as it came the minute the tests were over.

Perhaps it coincided with my wardrobe transition. One day I was wearing the size seven blue jeans that I'd worn since ninth grade, and the next, I couldn't zip those buggers up for all the fudge-covered Oreos this side of Omaha. I was simply forced to leave them unzipped. I did, however, rig up a closing mechanism by looping one of my hair elastics through the button hole that could fasten to the button on the other side—quite resourceful, if you ask me, and necessary if I didn't want to lose my drawers in public. Of course, this required that I wear a rather long shirt to cover the gaping—and bulging—V-shaped space where my zipper wouldn't close.

Yes, it was some time during this wardrobe-rigging phase of my pregnancy that I realized I had turned almost human again. When I woke up, I actually felt like eating breakfast—what a concept. The nausea and constant fatigue had skipped town leaving behind a voracious appetite—and for some pretty crazy stuff, I might add—as well as a newly bulging belly.

This whole weight gaining issue was a tad disconcerting, however. If I hadn't known it was my very own developing child causing my waistline to expand like your average hot air balloon getting ready to cross the North Atlantic, I'm sure I would have freaked a bit and purchased a year's supply of Slim Fast shakes. But this wasn't a time for dieting, this was a time for growth and transition; a time of joy and creation; the celebration of new life.

So why couldn't I quit crying?

Perhaps because, at the moment, the only items of clothing in my entire closet that I fit into belonged to *my husband*—the guy who was a head taller than me and generally weighed at least forty pounds more than me—at least I *hoped* he still did. The whole situation just wasn't right.

As I stood in front of the bathroom mirror staring at myself dressed in a pair of Gordon's jeans (with the legs rolled up) and wearing one of his plain white T-shirts to cover my growing mid-section, a fresh wave of emotion overcame me and the tears fell freely. *So this was my reality—swapping clothes with my husband! What was next, raiding Curt's closet?* This thought only brought on more tears. *Oh, life could be so cruel!*

A knock at the door sent me scrambling to dry my face on the bath towel hanging from the shower curtain's rod. After a quick glance in the mirror to confirm what I already knew (my eyes were puffy and red, and my nose was running), I made my way into the living room, up the stairs, and opened the door.

All it took was one look at Amy's concerned expression as she stood outside our basement apartment bundled in her winter coat, and I was once again awash in tears—and not just your basic little boo-hoo. I was an ugly, snorting, nose-dripping mess of muddled female hormones and nothing short of a shopping spree or a mound of greasy, salted french fries drenched in fry sauce could console my grief.

"What's wrong?" Amy nearly shrieked. "Are you okay?"

I left the door open, turned, and ran back down the stairs hoping that my friend would follow me. She did.

When we reached the living room, I raced to the couch and threw the entire weight of my body on its cushions. I *was* mindful, however, to land on my side. As much as I wanted to make a dramatic statement, as well as wallow fully and completely in my misery, I certainly didn't want to injure my unborn child with the ever increasing weight of my body. This thought alone sent another howl escaping from my lips.

"Did you and Gordon have a fight?" Amy asked with concern as she sat on the edge of the couch gently patting my back.

I lifted my face from the couch pillow and turned it to the side before responding, partly so Amy could hear and understand what

I was trying to say but mostly because it's actually quite difficult to breathe, let alone cry, when your face is jammed into the center of a cushy pillow.

"Gordon's not even heeeeere," I wailed.

"What about Curt?" Amy asked as she continued to pat.

I spoke between sobbing gasps that for some reason seem to be uncontrollable when you're crying hysterically. "They both went to help someone move, with the Elder's Quorum."

Amy's voice softened a bit. "Well, that's nice that the guys are doing volunteer work for the elderly on a Saturday morning, but that doesn't tell me why you're falling apart."

When Amy said this, I rolled over onto my back and started to laugh, well, between sobs. And that made me snort, which made me laugh even harder.

Amy stared at me like I was out of my mind as I continued this maniacal behavior of half crying, half laughing. She eventually put her hand to my forehead.

"Are you okay?"

With that, I stood up, lifted my hands out to each side and spun around.

"Do I look okay?" I said. Now I was crying again. Maybe even worse than before—it was hard to tell.

"Well, I'm not sure how to answer," Amy said, as she slowly leaned back onto the couch. "Is this some sort of trick question 'cause I'm just a little worried that you'll wig out and fall off the deep end no matter what I say."

"Look at me, Amy." I pulled out on the sides of my husband's jeans. "I'm wearing Gordon's clothes. I no longer fit into *any* of my clothes—and I'm *hu-u-u-u-uge!*" I was crying again, and through my sobs I'd managed to add four more syllables to the word "huge."

Amy stood up, walked toward me and took me in her arms, once again, patting my back while speaking calmly, as if soothing the fears of a little child.

"Hush now. It's okay. It's okay."

"No, it's not." I sobbed into Amy's shoulder. "I wear the same size pants as my huuusband."

Amy suddenly gripped my upper arms and held me back, looking into my eyes. "You know, there *is* a solution for this."

"What?"

"Maternity clothes."

You'd have thought she said "chocolate" by the calming expression that came over me.

"But money's so tight for us right now," I protested.

"No. Your *clothes* are tight right now," Amy clarified. "Besides, Gordon doesn't want you to be miserable like this."

"You know, I didn't even know I was until I tried on Gordon's pants this morning," I said as I wiped at my eyes with the bottom of my, I mean Gordon's, T-shirt. "No one should *ever* try on her husbands pants—even if she's pregnant. 'Cause if they fit, it's just way too depressing."

"Yeah," Amy agreed. "So let's go shopping—get you some things that fit."

After looking in the checkbook, I realized that we'd probably survive if I spent a little on maternity clothes. Besides, it was inevitable. I was almost five months pregnant now. And I certainly wasn't about to raid Curt's closet!

❈❈❈

I'm not sure why, but there's just something about wandering through those sliding double doors of any given Wal-Mart that manages to lift my spirits in a way that can only compare to eating dinner at one of my favorite restaurants, or perhaps Christmas morning. It's totally inexplicable but obviously a phenomenon that isn't exclusive to little ol' me.

Within an hour of entering my beloved shopping center of choice, I'd transformed into an entirely new person, both physically and emotionally. I even *felt* kinda cute. Amy and I found so many adorable outfits. Never in my life had I realized that pregnant women could look so fashionable. It wasn't necessary for us to rig our clothing or raid our husbands' closets. What had I been thinking?

There were so many darling outfits in the store, I could have easily spent an entire month of rent on a new wardrobe. But since I didn't think Gordon would be too pleased with this idea, I opted for two pairs of maternity pants (one black and the other made out of a stretchy denim-like material) and two shirts. I was good to go!

"I'm starved," I said as Amy and I headed out to the Wal-Mart parking lot.

"Me too," Amy replied. "What are our options?"

I quickly glanced into my wallet. "I don't dare take another penny out of the checking account, but I do have, let's see," I pulled everything silver from my coin purse as well as a rumpled-up dollar bill. "I have two dollars and sixty-five cents, plus at least a dozen pennies."

Amy did a similar assessment of her finances. "I have seven dollars and twenty-two cents, but this has to last me until I fly home Thursday after finals."

"We can go back to The Cave and have ramen noodles or peanut butter and jelly."

Amy scrunched up her nose. "Nah, we need to have a celebration feast."

"What are we celebrating? Finals next week?"

"It's too soon for that. Besides, we don't want to jinx anything."

I wanted to laugh at Amy because the last time I used the word "jinx" I think I was eleven—maybe twelve. But I used restraint (something I had been incapable of earlier in the morning).

"Then what?"

"We're celebrating your two new outfits," Amy spoke as if this idea was the most natural thought in the universe. Who was I to question this?

"Sounds good to me."

Within a matter of minutes, the two of us were sitting in a booth at Arctic Circle. A mound of french fries was piled in the middle of the table and little tubs of fry sauce dotted the perimeter. Life was good.

We dipped and munched in silence, simply enjoying the moment. Finally, after taking a sip of my ice water, I spoke.

"So tell me, what's really going on between you and Curt? I can't decide if you're just pals, or if there's more to it. The chemistry between the two of you always seems to be there, but one minute you're holding hands and the next you just seem like you're only pals or something."

Amy took a long swig of her ice water before speaking. "I've been wondering about this myself for the past few months. Sometimes I just can't figure your brother out."

"Yeah, me either," I replied as I popped another fry into my mouth.

"I sure wish I knew what was going on inside of his head. Sometimes I think he really might want a serious relationship, and but then other times he seems like something's holding him back."

"Yeah, well actually, I have a good idea what that is."

Amy had been dipping a fry in the sauce but now held it up as she spoke, oblivious that it was dripping on the table. "What?"

"He's trying to get ready to serve a mission for our church when the school year ends—a two-year mission." I paused, trying to let my words sink in. "Remember? We talked about it up at City of Rocks that one day when we were hiking. I'm surprised Curt hasn't mentioned it any more to you."

"He hasn't," she said, almost to herself.

"If he were to become seriously involved with you he might risk delaying his mission. He may even be worried that he might change his mind about going."

"And that would be a bad thing?" Amy asked.

Wow. I hadn't expected our "celebration feast" to take this turn and to be honest, I was more than a little irritated with my brother at the moment for not discussing all of this with Amy, his nonmember, more-often-than-not, somewhat-of-a girlfriend.

I took a deep breath and said a little prayer in my heart before I continued. "Amy, this may be hard for you to understand because you're not a member of our church, but actually, it's a commandment for all worthy nineteen-year-old boys in our church to serve a two-year mission."

"Seriously?"

"Yep. And, actually, it's a really great thing. Gordon served a mission and swears that it was the best two years of his life—well, before he met me, anyway. And my dad and our two older brothers, Alex and Blake, served missions as well. I've been able to see firsthand what a blessing it has been for them, as well as their families, and how they grew in so many ways over that two year period."

"And what if Curt decided not to go?" Amy asked.

I thought quite a bit about Amy's question before I replied because there really wasn't an easy answer. I only hoped and prayed that I'd say the right thing.

"Well, not only would he miss out on an incredible opportunity—one that would help him grow not only spiritually but also in many other ways as well—but I'm sure my parents and the rest of the family would also be somewhat disappointed. I also think Curt would eventually regret it."

Amy didn't respond. She seemed lost in thought as she repeatedly stirred the tip of a french fry in the sauce.

"I'm not really sure what else to tell you, Amy. Curt's really the one you ought to be talking to about this."

She finally responded with a forced smile. "Yeah, I suppose."

"Amy?"

"Yeah."

I almost hated to ask the following question, since the answer seemed obvious, but I felt that I needed to know.

"What do you think Curt should do?"

Amy seemed to wait forever before responding, but when she did, she looked me straight in the eye, and I could tell she was having difficulty keeping her emotions in check. "To be honest, Molly, I can't even think straight right now. All I know for certain is that I'm falling in love with your brother more and more each day and can hardly stand the thought of being away from him for Christmas break, let alone the next two years."

At first I didn't know what to say to that, but I did know a few things relating to matters of the heart. I reached out and took Amy's hand in mine and gave it a little squeeze. "You're a pretty amazing person, Amy. I know in the past you've warned me about getting all religious on you, but I can promise you one thing if you'll bear with me. Heavenly Father does hear and answer everyone's prayers—my prayers, Curt's prayers, and even *your* prayers. I know that if you ask Him for help, he'll get you through this. I promise you that."

I half expected Amy to laugh at me, but she didn't. She simply looked into my eyes for a few moments before responding in a soft, somber voice.

"Thanks, Molly."

Chapter
FIFTEEN

As I walked out of my economics class—my final final, so to speak—I felt like doing cartwheels, or even letting out a big whoop right there in Graveley Hall. But, I forced myself to show some restraint. Besides, with my newly developed "baby bulge," my tumbling days were certainly a thing of the past—or possibly even the future. But, definitely not something I could, would, or should attempt at the present.

It was Thursday afternoon and the campus of Idaho State University seemed almost abandoned. Gordon had taken his last final exam on Wednesday and had agreed to work full-time at the grocery store up until the start of the spring semester (aside from a three day Christmas break).

I continually had to remind myself that this was a *good* thing since we really needed the income, but it would be lonely as well. Amy was flying out that afternoon for Tulsa. The plan was for Curt to drop her off at the Pocatello Regional Airport on his way home to Oakley. I looked at my watch and realized they were probably at the airport right now. Since he'd taken Old Blue, my ancient pickup truck, I was forced to trek home in the snow on foot. It wasn't deep, but the air was cold, and I was heading toward an empty apartment. If it weren't for my elation that finals were over, I'm sure I'd have been just a bit depressed.

As I was walking past the Reed Gym, I found myself subconsciously turning toward the facility's main entrance. Not so much because I wanted to reminisce about my brief stint as a member of the ISU women's basketball team, but because I really needed to use the bathroom—an ever increasing event in my rapidly changing life.

Halfway to the women's locker room, I noticed a tall, blond guy walking from the opposite end of the corridor toward me. I knew exactly who it was. The good looks of Chad Hanks were quite discernible—even from the opposite end of a long hall. At this point, turning around wasn't really an option unless I wanted to look like a coward or worse yet, risk an unfortunate accident on the way home—no thanks! But I certainly didn't want to face Chad, even in passing. The guy ranked next to terrorists and obnoxiously loud movie-goers on my not-so-favorite people list.

My only hope was that somehow he wouldn't recognize me as we passed (after all, I *had* gained a bit of baby-fat over the past few months). I knew I was out of luck, however, when I made the mistake of looking up and into his blue eyes. They were staring directly at me—reading my innermost thoughts. But with our history, I guess it wouldn't take any genius for him to figure just which planet in the solar system I wished he'd be transported to. It was no secret, even to Chad himself, that unlike most people (who probably didn't know the guy personally), I was not a fan. He may have Gordon fooled but not me.

I could tell by his expression that it was an awkward moment for him as well, and I must admit to feeling just a hint of satisfaction in this thought. He *should* feel uncomfortable around me. I *wanted* him to squirm a little in his own skin when he looked into my laser gun eyes. The guy deserved it after what he did to Shannon, one of the dearest people in my life.

I practically held my breath as we passed—I think he did to. Neither of us offered a verbal greeting; a simple nod of recognition was all the guy would get out of me (and he was lucky for that). If I were to show my true feelings, I would have elbowed, or even tripped him in passing, but the thought would have to remain one of my little unfulfilled fantasies.

A sense of relief swept through me when we finally passed each other. Another unpleasant situation avoided. I could proceed with the task at hand.

"Molly?"

My stomach fell—figuratively, of course—when I heard Chad call my name from behind. Slowly, I stopped walking, let out a deep breath and rotated in my spot. I folded my arms in front of me—a barrier, I suppose, to keep this little reunion of sorts from getting too amicable (like that was even a remote possibility).

Chad slowly approached, and I must admit to feeling a sense of contentment in his apprehensiveness. Could the guy possibly even know how much I disliked him?

"Hey," he finally said when we were at a decent conversation's length away from each other.

I gave a terse nod.

After a brief moment of awkwardness, Chad made another attempt to converse. I could tell by the way he was shifting his weight from one foot to another that he was terribly uncomfortable with this situation. I had to wonder why he even bothered to pursue whatever it was that he was up to. What did he hope to achieve from having a conversation with me? I suppose I had to give the guy an A for effort, or stupidity. I wasn't sure yet.

Chad continued on, albeit hesitantly. "Um, ever since I saw you back in the math lab that one day at the beginning of the semester, I've wanted to talk to you, but, well, it's kind of an awkward situation."

I didn't respond, just continued to meet his gaze with my own. Honestly, I didn't want to give this guy an inch. After all he did to Shannon back in high school, why should I attempt to make this any easier on him.

"I guess I was just wondering how Shannon's doing. If she's, you know, okay?"

I let out a brief chuckle that held little trace of humor as I spoke. "Wow, I'm touched that you're even *remotely* concerned with anything having to do with my cousin. I guess life's full of surprises, isn't it?"

Chad let out a deep breath. But instead of getting defensive, which is what I expected, his countenance seemed to fall even more. If I hadn't disliked the guy so much I might have almost felt bad.

"I understand she's married now."

"Yep, and to a really great guy—which is what she deserves after all she's been through."

Chad's gaze fell to the ground for several seconds and when he looked back up into my eyes it was hard to read his facial expression except for the slight nodding of his head. Was he agreeing with me or humoring me?

"I was wondering if, well, um, I'd really like to speak with her in person, just for a few minutes. But I'm not sure how to go about it. I was wondering, Molly, if you might be able to help me?"

"Didn't you hear what I said? She's married. She's even pregnant."
I wanted to say "again", but I didn't.

"I just want . . . I just need to talk to her, only for a minute." Now
Chad was starting to look a little desperate. "Do you know if she'll be
in Oakley for Christmas?"

I knew for certain that Shannon and Justin would be back home
for the holidays because we'd just talked on the phone a few days earlier about the four of us getting together (and showing off our pregnant bellies, of course). But I wasn't quite sure what Chad was up to.
I needed to talk to my cousin and feel out the situation before I gave
him any information. I didn't trust the guy at all.

"Look, Chad, I don't know what you're up to, but you really should
just leave Shannon alone; she's happy with her life right now. Let's
keep it that way, okay?"

I'd had about enough of this conversation, and so had my bladder,
so I turned to head back down the hall.

Chad's voice managed to follow me, almost knocking me over—
not by its force but by the depth of emotion I felt in it. "I need to . . . I
have to apologize to her."

At some point my feet stopped walking and I slowly turned back
around, but I found myself with nothing to say.

"I need to do this, Molly." Chad's voice was weary. "I really need
your help."

I wanted to believe the guy. And something deep down in my
heart even told me that I probably should. But for some reason, my
mind wouldn't let me do it. The memories of the past were still too
vivid, still too painful, and I hadn't even been the one directly af-
fected.

"I'll talk to her," was all I said before turning and walking away,
but all I could think was that Chad Hanks didn't deserve Shannon's
forgiveness.

❊❊❊

Who says you can't celebrate alone? I had just spent a horrific
week spewing forth every ounce of knowledge that my pregnant brain
cells could possibly hold without spontaneously combusting. Now, I
was going to have a little party—even if it was all by myself. Besides,
after my earlier encounter in the gym with Chad, I was in desperate
need of a mood altering substance—chocolate!

So when I sat down in front of the television with my TV/VCR remote in hand and kicked up my feet onto the coffee table between a plate of nachos dripping with melted cheese sauce, and an unopened box of fudge-covered Oreos, situated next to a tall glass of milk, I knew the detour to the mini-mart had been inspired. With a twitch of my thumb, I'd be watching some of my favorite movies of all time— *Seven Brides for Seven Brothers*, and *Sleepless in Seattle*, for starters. If Gordon found me passed out on the couch at 1 A.M. with fudge stains on my fingers, cheese sauce dripping from my chin, and a young Julie Andrews singing *Do Re Mi*, to the sound of my snoring, so be it! I was having a one woman party and I deserved it—guilt need not attend.

Just as Millie was about to take off to the hills with Adam, the handsome backwoodsman, I was jerked away from my movie by the sound of my brother's voice as he opened The Cave door, and he descended the stairs.

"Molly!" It was more of a holler than anything.

"I'm right here," I said with my mouth half-full of nachos. "You don't have to scream."

"I don't?" Curt replied as he rounded the stairs and glared down upon me and my little finals feast.

"My hearing's perfect—and so are these nachos—want some?" I held up my half-eaten plate. "There's more in the kitchen."

I wanted to ask why he was back here in Pocatello and not halfway home to Oakley by now. But I could see that my brother was upset and I figured that at the moment, an offering of food would go over better than anything else—especially twenty questions from me.

Curt didn't look hungry—well, except for that familiar expression I'd seen a million times throughout our childhood indicating that he was ready to chew my head off.

"What did you say to her?" he nearly yelled.

"What? What are you talking about?"

"You know what I'm talking about." He exploded. "What did you say to Amy before she left?"

I began to search my brain for some sort of understanding. This simply wasn't like Curt to act this way. Something must have gone terribly wrong at the airport.

"I told her goodbye, to have a great Christmas, and to call me at Mom and Dad's."

Curt remained in place but now with his arms folded in front of him. "I just left the airport, after dropping Amy off, and she told me that after talking to *you* she now has a 'better understanding of things.' She told me when she comes back after Christmas we probably shouldn't see each other any more. Well, except for maybe when she's here visiting you. What the heck's going on here, Molly? What did you say to her?"

I must admit, I was in a bit of a shock from Curt's sudden appearance and outburst. Frantically, I tried to recall the most recent conversation I'd had with Amy. What *had* I said?

An image of me and Amy sitting in a booth at Arctic Circle, dipping our fries in fry sauce popped to the forefront of my memory. My own words seemed to twirl randomly around in my brain.

"If he were to become seriously involved with you he might risk delaying his mission . . . He may even be worried that he might change his mind about going . . . I'm sure my parents and the rest of the family would be somewhat disappointed . . . I also think Curt would eventually regret it."

Curt must have detected a guilty expression on my face, because I definitely recognized fury in his. "For once in your life, Molly, why can't you just mind your own business? Who gave you permission to direct the people who come in and out of my life?"

I wanted to respond—to tell Curt that I hadn't meant any harm. I was only trying to help explain the whole mission thing to Amy because I loved him and wanted the best for him—but I didn't have a chance. As fast as my brother entered, he left, leaving nothing behind but his anger.

What had I done?

Chapter
SIXTEEN

I couldn't be certain of the driving force. Perhaps, I'd been watching a little too much HGTV. Or maybe, I was feeling some sort of Relief Society peer pressure intensified by pregnancy hormones. It certainly didn't help that Christmas was around the corner and we were on a very tight budget. But whatever the cause, during my brief hiatus from school for the holiday season, I found myself in an arts and crafts frenzy. If I wasn't concocting scrumptious holiday morsels to share with our visiting and home teaching routes (as well as fulfilling my own cravings), I was painting, sewing, stamping, or gluing. Whether it was financially or hormonally driven, I'm not sure, but I was in an all-out battle against store-bought gifts.

Armed with my trusty glue gun, the sewing machine my grandma had given me when I graduated from high school, a tole painting kit I'd assembled in seventh grade, and perhaps even with delusions of being the new Martha Stewart, I was a woman on a mission. I had nothing but time on my hands and paint under my fingernails. It would be homemade gifts for everyone on my list this year, or I'd glue my fingers together trying. That's how committed—or insane—I was.

As I was in the middle of hot-gluing a beard onto a wooden, tole-painted Santa Claus, the phone rang and I was forced to leave my Santa looking scandalously half-shaved, to answer it.

"Hey, how's my favorite cousin?" Shannon's voice sounded so upbeat.

"I'm on a craft binge—all homemade gifts this year."

"Wow—Grandma'll be so proud."

I knew Shannon was right. Grandma hadn't given a store-bought Christmas gift in her entire mortal existence. The woman was freakishly clever with yarn and could perform miracles with left-over fabric scraps. Everyone was in awe of her homemade gifts—and sometimes afraid.

"Are you making us matching maternity dresses?" Shannon asked.

"Should I?"

"No. Please . . . no more matching dresses. Grandma would love it, but I think it was a positive move on our part when we gave them up ten years ago."

"Well, good, 'cause I'm better with a glue gun than a sewing machine." It felt so great to be chatting with Shannon again. The girl probably understood me better than anyone in the entire universe—including my beloved goofball husband.

"Just don't burn yourself," Shannon warned.

"Are you referring to the glue gun or my life in general at the moment?"

"What's that supposed to mean?"

"It means that I'm in hot water with Curt and probably my friend Amy as well, who happens to sorta be Curt's girlfriend, or at least she was until I told her about Curt's mission plans."

"What's wrong with that?" said Shannon. "It's not a secret is it?"

"No, it's not—I guess. It's just that she told him they probably shouldn't see each other any more"

"He may be angry now, Molly, but I bet he thanks you down the road. You're just looking out for his best interest, right?"

"Absolutely." I was trying to convince myself. "I'm his big sister. It's my job."

"So don't worry about it. Curt's resilient. He'll move forward." Shannon voice sounded convincing, but deep down I had a feeling that it wasn't going to be that simple.

I was somewhat relieved when Shannon changed the subject. "How long are you and Gordon going to be in Oakley for Christmas?"

"Only three days. Gordon has to work."

"Well, we *have* to get together. Maybe Christmas Eve. I can't wait to see your belly."

When Shannon mentioned getting together, I couldn't help but remember my unfortunate encounter with Chad only a week earlier. He'd wanted me to talk to Shannon, I guess to smooth the way for him. He claimed he wanted to apologize, but I questioned the guy's sincerity. Besides, Shannon had moved on with her life. She was happy. Why should she have to endure dirt from her past being dug up and thrown back into her face? I decided right then and there, that I wouldn't tell her about my conversation with Chad. He could just live with his mistakes. I was only concerned with looking out for Shannon's best interest.

"Christmas Eve sounds great," I finally replied. "And I bet my belly's bigger than yours."

Shannon half snorted. "I seriously doubt that. The only things that fit me any more are my sweat pants."

"Well whatever you do, don't try on Justin's pants."

"I'll try to resist."

"You have to. Just trust me on this one."

"Molly, married life hasn't changed you a bit. You're still strange."

"I try," I replied. "Hey, I'll call you when we get there, okay?"

After hanging up, I headed back to the task at hand—hot-gluing the rest of Santa's beard on. I couldn't seem to concentrate, however. Probably because the events of the previous week began to whirl around in my mind.

I hadn't talked to Curt since he stormed out of The Cave a week earlier. My hope was that a little time and distance would calm down his fury. I'd called Amy after she arrived home, but she sounded a bit distant—and I'm not referring to the miles between Oklahoma and Idaho. She just wasn't her usual animated self.

Then there was this business with Chad. Why did life have to be so complicated? And how did I always end up in the middle of everyone else's messes?

※※※

It was the day before we were leaving for Oakley—December 23, to be exact—and my "to do" list was almost complete. I'd made and wrapped all of my gifts, sent out Christmas cards (handmade, of course), and we were all packed and ready to leave for Oakley as soon as Gordon got off of work. There was only one thing left to do, and I wasn't sure if I was excited or terrified about it.

I'd always heard about women having an ultrasound procedure during their pregnancy. Well, today it was my turn. Every pregnant woman I knew had gotten an ultrasound, and they didn't seem to shudder when talking about the experience (as opposed to labor and delivery), so I figured I should save my worries for the big stuff still ahead.

My appointment with the radiology department at Bannock Regional Medical Center was scheduled for 1 P.M. with strict instructions to drink several glasses of water prior to the appointment. Apparently this would allow the ultrasound technician to take a better peek at the little tyke in my belly who lately felt like he or she had taken up hockey or the hula.

The catch, however, was that you couldn't use the bathroom until the procedure was over. Easy enough, right? I was a big girl. If I could run a 10K, play collegiate level basketball, and do five hundred crunches, I could certainly deal with a full bladder.

So I hadn't worried too much about those three tall glasses of water I'd chugged before coming to the hospital until I was sitting in the lobby, waiting for Gordon to arrive and for the lady at the desk to call my name. It was at this point, however, when I realized that there might be a problem.

There were at least a dozen other people also waiting in the rows of chairs for some sort of X-ray or ultrasound procedure, and I began to wonder just how long this might take. To ease my ever increasing discomfort, I stood up, crossed my ankles and propped one shoulder against the wall.

"Hey there, pretty lady," came that ever familiar voice from behind me. When I turned to face Gordon, he had a can of soda in one hand as he pulled me close with the other. I was afraid to hug him too tight, afraid I might burst.

When we pulled apart I couldn't help but eye that can of soda as if it were the enemy. I then shifted my stare toward my unsuspecting husband.

"You thirsty?" he asked with raised eyebrows, offering the can to me.

"Gordon!" I nearly shrieked.

"What?"

I tried my best to lower my voice. "I'm about to wet my pants, and you come in here with *that*. Why don't you just get a nurse and have her start an IV drip in the back of my hand, for Pete's sake."

"I'm sorry. It's my lunch hour. I had to wash my peanut butter sandwich down with something."

My voice softened. "I know, I'm sorry. I'm just a little on edge." I crossed my ankles again, as well as locking my knees together, hoping I didn't look too conspicuous. What was my alternative? "I don't know how much longer I can wait."

A concerned look spread across Gordon's face. "Let me see what's taking so long." Gordon Nelson—my hero!

Gordon approached the desk, talked to the lady for a few seconds and then pointed at me. I gave a lame little wave of my fingers and a half smile, but that was all I could manage. The situation was getting serious.

When Gordon came back, he propped one hand against the wall. "It's only going to be about five more minutes. She said you can go use the bathroom but only a little bit."

"What? What's that supposed to mean?"

Gordon just shrugged.

I wanted to cry, and if I thought it would have helped, I probably would have.

The lady at the desk called another name, and an elderly lady and her husband stood up and followed the nurse through the double doors. I bet *she* hadn't been asked to drink the entire contents of Lake Erie and then try to hold her bladder for a million years, or worse yet, empty it just a little bit. That's like telling someone it's okay to sneeze but just a little. Not possible! At least not for me. Where's the humanity?

Gordon stood next to me in silence, offering his moral support by holding my hand. I was grateful that he'd been able to take a late lunch from the grocery store to be with me here for this big event in our lives. I just wished I'd been in a little better state of mind, and body. But I wasn't. The last time I had to use the bathroom this bad, it was at the end of my first day of kindergarten. And I would have made it home dry if that darn bus hadn't been so bumpy.

The following day my Mom dropped me off at school and we did a thorough tour together of the restroom facilities at Oakley Elementary School. That was the last time I'd wet my pants. I hoped today wouldn't change all that.

"Molly Nelson."

I wanted to jump up and scream, "Here!", but any sudden movements—especially jumping—were definitely out of the question.

In a matter of minutes I found myself wearing a hospital gown and lying on an exam table in a dimly lit room with a blanket over my legs. I was relieved when the ultrasound technician walked in and introduced herself. Her name was Megan and she looked like she could be my mom. Despite my doctor phobia, she was able to put me at ease.

"I'm just going to squirt a little of this gel on your belly and take a few pictures," said Megan.

I was pleasantly surprised that the gel was actually warm. Megan turned off the lights so the only thing illuminating the room was something that looked like a computer monitor.

She began moving the rounded instrument across my stomach with one hand while unusual fuzzy grey images began swirling around the monitor. Every few seconds she'd hit a key on the computer keyboard with her other hand and the image would freeze. With precision, she'd mark certain points on the image, type in a few words or numbers, and then hit another key so the swaying, fuzzy grey would reappear. I had no clue what I was looking at, but obviously she did.

"How do you make heads or tails of all this?" Gordon spoke in a hushed tone.

"I've been doing this for a dozen years," Megan replied. "We actually get quite a bit of information from the ultrasound."

"Can you tell if it's a boy or a girl?" asked Gordon.

"Usually."

Gordon leaned over toward my ear. "Do you want to know what it is?"

"Yeah," I whispered.

"I'll let you know what I can see," said Megan, obviously overhearing our conversation.

She continued to move the instrument around until she hit a certain spot low on my abdomen. "See that? She said pointing with her finger to a little pulsating blob on the monitor. There's a heartbeat."

And she was right. There was my baby's tiny little blob-like heart, ticking away like a little clock. *Incredible!*

I no longer had thoughts about my need to use the restroom, homemade Christmas gifts, or the numerous frustrations in my life regarding the "Curt and Amy" situation or even Chad Hanks.

My baby's heart was beating. And mine had swelled to, well, the size of a mother's heart. Nothing in the universe could ever be bigger—fuller.

I didn't realize that tears were sliding down the side of my face until I felt Gordon's finger wiping away the moisture. Then I felt his lips against my cheek. "Hey, Mommy, you doing okay?" he whispered.

I just nodded, and then reached up to take his hand.

Megan continued to move the instrument around my belly while we stared intently at the fuzzy grey screen, hoping for some sort of discernable image of our child. After a few moments, her words broke into the sweet quiet. "Well, look at that," she said with a slight chuckle.

"What?" Gordon and I replied unanimously.

"I thought you looked kinda big."

I wanted to say, "Excuse me?" but didn't get a chance because Megan continued, "Looks like we've got some company."

"What do you mean?" Gordon asked.

Megan's smile grew as she maneuvered the instrument around. "See this," she said, pointing to the monitor.

I was nodding, and Gordon verbalized my thoughts. "Yeah."

"That's a heartbeat. *Another* heartbeat." She paused to let her words sink in. "Congratulations, Mr. and Mrs. Nelson. You're having twins, and at least one of them is a boy."

Chapter
SEVENTEEN

If I was feeling a bit insecure about motherhood BU (Before Ultrasound), I was feeling nothing short of panic now. What was Heavenly Father thinking, anyway? He certainly must have a sense of humor, that's for sure. I wished at the moment that I could find mine. But I'd lost it months ago between bouts of early morning nausea and midnight heartburn. Where's the humor in heartburn?

Didn't Heavenly Father realize that I'm a one-at-a-time kind of gal? I don't even like mixed vegetables. I'm also not good at multi-tasking—never have been. I can't drive and talk on the cell phone. I can't even read and eat at the same time. How in the world am I supposed to handle two newborn babies, when the mere thought of being solely responsible for even one infant brings about hives on my neck and a distinct twitch to my left eye?

And then there's that whole getting-them-here issue. They'd have to come out eventually, right? That, in and of itself is completely terrifying. Sure, they were content right now to swim around and cuddle with each other. But just wait until spring when one will have its foot in the other one's ear. No doubt they'll be poking and kneeing each other (and me) in search of that pathway to freedom—or at least a little more elbow room. Could I deliver them naturally, or would they arrive via an opening created by a doctor's scalpel?

Where's a king-sized Symphony bar with almonds and toffee when you really need it?

My frenzied thoughts were momentarily interrupted as Gordon's hand reached out across the front seat of our rusty old Suburban to take mine. We were on our way to Oakley and it was already dark outside. The only illumination came from the moon and dashboard lights.

"My Molly's being awfully quiet," said Gordon. His fingers interlocked with mine and I could slowly feel my body relax to his touch.

"Well, my thoughts aren't being quiet," I confessed. "You should hear the commotion going on inside my head. On second thought, maybe you shouldn't"

"Yeah, I should. I really want to know how you're feeling about all of this—about the twins."

I sat in silence for a moment, took a deep breath, and then plunged in to my thoughts of inadequacy and fear. I figured Gordon would tell me that I'd be just fine and not to worry, but I was surprised when he took the conversation in a different direction.

"I don't presume to understand what you might be feeling right now, Molly." Gordon gave my hand a little squeeze before continuing. "But I *do* understand fear and self-doubt."

"Really? You've always come across to me as confident—self-assured."

"Not always." Gordon chuckled. "When I decided to serve a mission, I'd only been a member of the Church for about three years. Aside from knowing that I was keeping a commandment, I was basically clueless about what I was getting into. The only missionaries I ever really knew were the ones that taught me the discussions when I was sixteen. And I must admit, I wanted to be just like them—to speak with that same spirit and testimony."

"You do. I've heard you speak in church. I've heard you bear your testimony."

"Yeah, sure. Now I can. But as a nineteen-year-old convert to the Church, I was terrified."

"Really?" This was all news to me. I'd never seen my husband as anything but confident since the day we met (okay, except for when he proposed to me, but we won't go there).

"When I entered the MTC and attempted to absorb all the information it was like trying to take a drink out of a fire hydrant. Let's just say, it was all a bit overwhelming. I was certain that I was the least qualified missionary in the universe to go out and preach the gospel."

"So what did you do?"

"I did the only thing I could do—I prayed, a lot. And I took one step at a time."

"But that's just it! Heavenly Father is asking me to take *two* steps at a time. I'm not sure I can do that without tripping and landing flat on my face."

Gordon reached over to pull me in closer. I loved the security I felt in his arms.

"Aren't you forgetting something?" said Gordon.

"What?"

"Me." Gordon leaned over, quickly kissed the top of my head, and then spoke soothingly into my ear. "I'm here to help, Molly. I'm the father of these babies—I'm supposed to help. I *want* to help."

I looked over through the dim light of the dashboard into Gordon's face. His sincerity was evident in his expression as well as his voice.

Gordon continued. "Between the two of us—three when you count Heavenly Father, 'cause you know he wants us to ask for His help too—we can get through this. And you just watch me. I'm going to master the art of baby burping and diaper changing."

"Oh, now *that* I'd like to see," I nearly howled.

"You just watch. I can deal with a little stink."

"Yeah, but how about two little stinks?"

"Molly! I *wasn't* referring to the babies."

"Neither was I."

The laughter that came next was completely refreshing, and I realized that maybe I needed to chill out a bit, for my own sake as well as Gordon's. Underneath all that fear and insecurity, a part of me was actually excited. What female in the history of mankind has never daydreamed about having twins—dressing them alike, and naming them something cute like Brittney and Breanne or Justin and Jeremy.

"Do you like 'J' names?" I suddenly found myself asking. "You know—like Justin and Jeremy?"

"I suppose they're okay, if you don't mind having the same name as a half-dozen other boys in your kindergarten."

"Ya think?" I asked.

"I know. And you're forgetting something."

"What?"

"Jeremy might actually be Jenny . . . or Jessica. The ultrasound lady could only tell that one was a boy."

"Then I guess we'll have to be flexible," I replied.

We sat in silence for a while both of our brains ticking away like the tiny little heartbeats we'd seen on the monitor earlier that day."

"I got it!" Gordon shouted, sending me jumping on the bench seat of the Suburban.

"Got what?"

"The perfect name for our son—or at least one of them."

"What?"

"Nephi." Gordon sat up straight and proud, as if he'd just uncovered the cure for bad breath. "He's my favorite prophet in the Book of Mormon."

"Yeah, but Nephi—Nephi Nelson?"

"Uh-huh," he said with a quick nod.

"Why don't we just name him Tease-me Nelson, or My-parents-must-hate-me Nelson.

Gordon took on a determined expression. "Our babies names need to mean something—be significant, like names from the scriptures or our ancestry."

Actually, I knew Gordon felt this way because we'd had the baby name conversation back in our dating days. He was quite serious.

I tried to keep an open mind, but I also wanted to be reasonable. "Since you like names from the scriptures, then why not Joshua? Or maybe Matthew or Benjamin? I know—Daniel!"

"Overused." Gordon replied.

"Overused isn't necessarily a bad thing, Gordon."

"I got it! How about our dad's names?" The sincerity in his expression was almost scary.

"Norman and Leo?"

"Sure why not?"

I could see that we weren't getting anywhere, and Gordon's suggestions were going from awful to worse. "We still have four and a half months. Why don't we figure this out later?"

"That's fine, but I don't want to end up taking home Baby A and Baby B Nelson from the hospital because we can't decide on names."

"Don't worry." Now I was the one doing the reassuring. "We've got plenty of time. I'm sure we'll eventually agree on names. Besides, I bet we're going to get plenty of suggestions over the next few days."

"So when are you going to tell everyone about the twins?" Gordon asked.

"I don't know," I replied. "Things are a little complicated with my family."

"How?"

"Oh, you know my Dad, he'll probably pat you on the back for a half hour before coming up with a few fertility jokes in an attempt to embarrass the both of us—trust me, we can do without *that*. And Mom, she'll immediately start to cry, which will make me cry, and I'm just not up to it right now."

"Well, don't wait too long."

"Why?"

"'Cause I have a feeling we're going to need a few name suggestions."

"Yeah," I agreed. "A few dozen."

Chapter EIGHTEEN

While I was growing up, our four bedroom, two-story house on Marion Road seemed just the right size for a family of seven. Now Mom's biggest complaint was that with only Dusty left at home, the place almost felt abandoned—but not for the holidays. When you added spouses and grandchildren into the mix, the environment became quite cozy.

Alex and Tiffany, along with their two little ones drove down from Moscow where Alex was working on a master's degree at the University of Idaho. Blake, still the eligible bachelor, was up from Provo. And Curt hightailed it back from Pocatello after finishing his finals (Oh yeah, and after chewing me out. I was still a bit sore about that—He probably was too). That left me and Gordon. As usual, we were the last to arrive.

"Well, look who's here," Dad bellowed as we walked through the front door. Everyone who had been sitting in the living room descended upon us in the entryway, and at least a half dozen random hands began patting my bulging belly.

"Wow, Mol, you're huge!" Dusty exclaimed. Now this might be a statement that someone would want to hear if they were a movie or television star, a politician, or a sumo wrestler, but it's definitely not something an emotionally and hormonally unstable woman wants to hear.

Curt stifled a chuckle while Mom thumped Dusty on the back of his head.

"Ow!" he yelped, turning toward Mom and rubbing the sore spot. "Whatcha do that for?"

Mom didn't respond, just gave Dusty one of her looks that meant, *Beware 'cause you're about to cross the line and for your own good, you don't want to do that.* Reading Mom's expressions and body language was a necessity growing up in the Chamber's house. We'd all become pretty good at it over the years.

"He's right, I am huge," I laughed, trying to get my little brother off the hook. Besides, if I didn't laugh, I just might cry.

"You look absolutely radiant," Mom responded, pulling me into a tight hug.

"Let me grab that," Dad said, taking the suitcase from Gordon.

"Thanks, Brother Chambers," said Gordon.

"Please, call me Dad, or Norm. None of this 'Brother Chambers' stuff around here. Save that for church." Dad smiled at Gordon and then winked at me. Boy, I sure missed my dad's feeble attempts at humor.

Gordon looked a little sheepish, so I grabbed his hand and gave it a reassuring squeeze.

"Let's take these up to your room," said Dad, "and then maybe we can play a little Monopoly."

"Good grief, Norm, let the kids relax a bit."

"They've been sitting for an hour and a half. Besides, Molly loves Monopoly, right Mol?"

"It's my favorite," I replied.

"I thought I was your favorite?" Gordon said with a wounded expression.

I reached up and pulled on his neck until his ear was nearly touching my mouth. "You know you are," I whispered and then kissed his cheek.

"Hey, none of this mush," Dad interrupted, but his face was wearing a huge grin.

After Mom and Dad helped us deposit our things upstairs in my old bedroom, Mom turned toward me. "Oh, I almost forgot to tell you. Chad Hanks called a bit ago. He is staying out at his mom's place and wants you to call him. He said it's important."

I couldn't help but groan and roll my eyes. Mom didn't seem to notice because she was already headed downstairs, but Gordon was a bit more perceptive—perhaps because he and Chad were friends. Or maybe because it was totally weird for Chad Hanks, of all people, to be calling me.

"Do you know what he's calling about?" He asked me.

"Yeah, but I'm not going to call him back. The guy just needs to leave well enough alone."

"What's that supposed to mean? What does he want?"

"To bring up the past, which Shannon really doesn't need right now—trust me!"

"Wait, wait, wait—" Gordon was shaking his head. "You're not making sense."

I exhaled while running my hands through my hair, trying to ease the tension that had started to build. "I ran into Chad in the gym the last day of finals. He said he wants to apologize to Shannon. He wants me to arrange some sort of a meeting—smooth the way or something like that, I suppose." I threw my hands up into the air. "I say he's too late for that."

"Molly, this isn't your business."

"Exactly! So why does he keep asking me to help him get in touch with Shannon?"

"What I mean is, I don't think you should try to stop this from happening. If he wants to apologize, Molly, who are you to stand in his way?"

Gordon had spoken in a soft tone, but his words stung. My first instinct was to list the numerous reasons that I needed to 'stand in the way.' Gordon didn't understand all that Shannon had been through in high school or the years of healing that followed. He hadn't lived through that whole teen pregnancy ordeal. He had no clue.

I placed my hands on my hips and stood firm. "Don't you trust my judgment?"

Gordon slowly approached me and ran his hands down the sides of my arms until they reached my fingers, covering them with his own. His blue eyes locked into mine and the expression was one of love.

His voice was gentle and soft. "That's just it, Molly. You're *not* the judge."

Had these words been delivered by anyone else, and in any other way, I'm sure I would have argued my point until my tongue collapsed. But now, standing here with Gordon holding my hands, teaching me what I instantly recognized to be an eternal truth, there was no argument to be made.

After a long moment of silence, I finally spoke. "So, what do I do?"

"Why don't you start by calling him back?"

I let out a deep breath while Gordon pulled me into a hug. He knew, as well as I did, that this would be hard for me.

🏵🏵🏵

At a quarter to three I gave up any attempt of sleeping and slowly tiptoed (or waddled) downstairs, depending on which direction you were watching me from. Usually, I had no problem sleeping. Since the earliest days of my pregnancy, I'd been able to fall into bed, roll over and become comatose until nature called a few hours later. But tonight, I had too many thoughts churning in my brain. I simply *couldn't* sleep.

Tomorrow was Christmas Eve. And, like it or not, I had made arrangements for Chad to speak with Shannon. We were all going to meet here at Mom and Dad's place for "the big apology." I was still skeptical about the whole thing, but Gordon was right—it wasn't my place to try and prevent it. I just hoped that this wouldn't send Shannon back in her progress of healing from such a painful experience.

At the moment, the house was dark except for a little night light Mom always left on in the kitchen. Suddenly, it seemed to be beckoning my name. I hadn't realized I was hungry until I opened the fridge and beheld a box of cold pizza—*Bingo!* After grabbing a large piece with a thick crust and pouring a glass of milk, I walked to the basement door, opened it, and headed down to the family room to watch a little television. Surely, a full stomach and some *Nick at Night* could help me to get some sleep.

It was immediately evident, however, that I wasn't the only person in the house suffering from a case of insomnia. As I descended the stairs, the dialog and laugh track from an old sitcom became more discernible. The light from the television revealed that Curt, as usual, had beaten me to not only the pizza but the remote control.

"Great minds think alike," I said, as I approached the Lazy-boy (the recliner variety—not the little brother variety) and landed not-so-gracefully onto its cushions.

Curt (also considered a "lazy boy" at times), was lying on the couch, still staring at the TV screen as if he hadn't even noticed my grand waddling entrance. Eventually, however, he let out a weak grunting sound. Was that an acknowledgement of my presence, or did the guy have heartburn?

I took a bite of my cold pizza and spoke with my mouth full. "So you gonna talk to me, or ignore me the entire holiday?"

Another grunt—or was that a groan this time?

After a few more moments of silence, I'd had enough and decided to stir things up (one of my favorite hobbies, by the way).

"She's in love with you, ya know."

Curt looked over at me. I finally had his attention. "Why do you say that?"

"She told me that she was falling in love with you."

I took another bite of pizza while Curt sat up straight. "She did?"

"Yeah, and I think you're falling in love with her too."

"Why would you say that?"

"Do I look as dumb as a doughnut?" It was a rhetorical question and I was grateful my brother knew better than to try and answer it. "Why else would you be acting like I stole your favorite Ninja Turtle and flushed it down the toilet."

"I gave up Ninja Turtles for Power Rangers a long time ago," My brother spoke with a straight face, but I could tell that his attitude was softening a bit. I must admit, I was relieved. As irritating as the kid could be sometimes, I missed the playful banter and trivial conversations we'd always been able to share so effortlessly. At the moment, however, I felt like I needed to level with him.

"You need to talk to her, Curt. You need to let Amy know what's going on inside your head—what you're planning to do. She's tired of guessing."

"I've tried to call a couple of times, her mom just makes up excuses for her—'she's asleep,' 'she's shopping,' 'she's in the shower.' Why won't she talk to me? Why doesn't she want to see me any more?"

"Before we head down that road, just tell me one thing. Do you still plan to serve a mission in the spring?"

Curt's tone turned defensive. "Yes, of course I am. So what's that got to do with anything?"

The answers all seemed so logical in my brain, but for some reason Curt couldn't see them—couldn't see the relationship between his reluctance to level with Amy about his feelings for her, as well as his somewhat conflicting plan to serve a mission for the Church, and her decision to quit seeing him.

I thought about Curt's words and my conversation with Gordon earlier that evening. Why did I always end up in the middle of other people's dramas? I let out a deep breath.

"You know what? You need to figure this out for yourself, and *I* need to stay out of everyone else's business."

Curt seemed a little surprised by my response. And, I have to admit, so was I. It would be so easy right now for me to step in and smooth things over for Amy and Curt. But ultimately, that didn't solve the problem. Curt needed to back up his decisions with the proper actions and level with Amy—it was only fair.

"I'm not just playing games with her," said Curt, sounding just a little bit defensive. "I *do* have feelings for her—that's part of the problem."

I bit my tongue but couldn't resist giving my brother a reassuring nod.

"I just get to feeling so overwhelmed with it all—my feelings for Amy, and the reality that I'll be gone for two whole years. Then, to top it all off, she doesn't even understand why I would want to serve a mission. She doesn't understand the gospel."

"Sounds like you have some missionary work cut out for you *before* you enter the mission field."

For the first time that night I saw a slight smile on my brother's face—or was that a look of terror? Only my brother could be sure.

Chapter
NINETEEN

When I finally woke up on the morning of Christmas Eve, morning had almost turned into afternoon. The numbers on the clock read 11:37. I couldn't even remember the last time I had slept in so late. I had to admit, it felt pretty good.

Gordon's side of the bed was empty. Knowing my husband, he'd probably been up for hours. Even when he worked late nights at the grocery store, he still found it difficult to sleep in. Sometimes I wondered how the guy functioned.

As I rolled over onto my back, stretched, and then looked down at my protruding abdomen, I couldn't help but relive those exciting and terrifying moments the previous day during the ultrasound. Was I actually having twins—two babies?

I rubbed the palms of my hands in gentle circles over my belly as if my babies could feel the touch of my hands against their delicate skin. In spite of my initial panic (which I was pretty sure would come and go over the next eighteen or so years) I wanted my children to know how much they were loved and wanted.

I hadn't planned on twins. Heck, I could still hardly believe it. But it *was* true; I had photographic evidence to prove it.

Just then, a thought came rushing into my mind—the perfect way to reveal our twin surprise to my parents.

What a great idea!

❋❋❋

After Gordon and I made a last minute shopping trip into the Burley Wal-Mart, we headed home to help Mom with the Christmas Eve preparations. There were always pies to bake and presents to wrap, not to mention the fact that Shannon and Justin—and Chad—

were coming over. The first two for dinner and a little reunion, and then Chad for "the big apology." I was *not* looking forward to that part of our evening.

I had decided to no longer fight this idea, but to be honest, deep down inside of me, I didn't like it. I was still mad at Chad Hanks, and I suppose a part of me wanted to continue being mad at him for a long time. Did the guy even realize how much damage he'd helped to cause back in high school? I suppose he did—and wanted to finally clear his conscience. Too bad that in doing so, it didn't also erase the truckload of pain and anguish that Shannon had to endure.

But, I wasn't going to fight it. I wasn't the judge and it wasn't my business. All I needed to worry about was supporting my cousin at this time. And if Shannon needed a listening ear after tonight while she found it necessary to trash Chad Hanks and his feeble attempt to reconcile their past issues, then so be it. I'd be more than happy to offer my assistance (which could also include a lashing tongue, if necessary).

When the doorbell sounded at a little after 6 P.M., I knew exactly who it was. After running to the front door and throwing it open, I let out a heartfelt shriek of pure joy, which was reciprocated in equal exuberance and decibel by my dear friend and cousin, Shannon.

After a brief hug, I grabbed her arms, pulling her out of the cold night and into the warmer entryway where I held out her hands like a scarecrow.

"You look so cute!" I said, my tone rising with each word.

"So do you," she said, pulling me in for one more embrace. This time our bellies touched, making us both laugh.

It had been way too long since Shannon and I had seen each other. And though our lives were parallel in experience (we were both newlyweds, students, and pregnant), we were living in separate locations—not at all the adjoining farmhouses we'd envisioned during our countless sleepovers as children.

As Shannon and I stood in the entryway, oblivious to all else in an attempt to catch up on our lives, Gordon and Justin had already made it past the handshakes and back slaps and were headed toward the kitchen where Gordon and I had just placed some appetizers on the table.

"Now, when is your due date?" Shannon asked, looking at my belly that was noticeably larger than hers—at least to me.

"Come here," I whispered to Shannon, pulling her into the living room. "Can you keep a secret?"

"Of course," Shannon replied, sounding a bit irritated that I'd even asked such a question. "What's up?"

I looked around to make sure we were completely alone before speaking. "I just found out yesterday that I'm having twins." I practically mouthed the last word as if I said it out loud, it might not be true.

Shannon's eyes widened. "No."

I'm sure I looked like one of those dashboard doggies the way my head continued to bob up and down in a nodding motion. "One's a boy, and the other wants to surprise us."

"Wow, that's incredible," she said, taking a closer inspection of my bulging belly. "Does Gordon know yet?"

"Yeah, but Mom and Dad don't. I'm going to surprise them with the news in the morning."

Shannon pulled me into another hug. "I'm so excited for you."

"Thanks, I'm excited too—and a little terrified."

Shannon leaned back and patted her own belly. "I have my own surprise."

My eyes grew wide. "What?"

Shannon placed her hand on her stomach. "I'm having another girl." Her eyes glistened as she spoke.

"Oh, I'm so happy for you."

"Me too," Shannon said, blinking back the moisture. "It's almost like, like I've been given a second chance."

Now my eyes began to tear up as the two of us embraced yet again. Our special moment, however, was quickly squelched as our husbands (who obviously didn't understand the complexities of the pregnant female psyche), entered the living room.

"I dunno," said Gordon, slapping Justin on his back. "I think this calls for extreme measures."

Justin's expression looked a little perplexed.

"What would you think about doing the old two-week trade off with these gals?"

Justin still looked perplexed, but Shannon almost looked horrified. I, however, knew better.

"Molly can stay two weeks with you two up in Rexburg, and after that, Shannon can come down and spend the next two weeks with us.

That way these two don't have to endure such a difficult separation.
I mean, really now, look at them," Gordon nodded his head in our
direction as we sat hunched together on the couch with our watery
eyes and sniffling noses, "we're their husbands and I doubt we've received as many hugs in the last twenty-four hours as these two have
given each other in the last five minutes."

I looked up into Gordon's almost-pouting face. "Do you need a
hug?"

His grin said it all.

After a wonderful dinner, including the other members of my
family, the four of us headed back into the living room while the rest
of the gang went down to the family room to watch *It's a Wonderful
Life*—a Chambers family tradition on Christmas Eve.

The guys were a few steps ahead of us discussing the various
bowl games coming up so I took the moment to pull Shannon aside
before we reached the living room.

"Are you still okay with all of this—with Chad coming over?"

Shannon took a deep breath before speaking. "Well, I can't say
it'll be the most comfortable situation I've ever been in, but I must
admit, I'm a little curious about what he has to say."

"If you don't mind my asking, what does Justin think about all
this?"

Shannon glanced into the living room where the guys were chatting away like old buddies and smiled. "He's quite sensitive to my
feelings—doesn't want me to get hurt again. So that part of him is
apprehensive. But I think he's feeling pretty much the same way I
am—wants to hear what Chad has to say."

"And you're going to be okay? 'Cause you know I can answer that
door when he knocks and tell the guy to get lost. It'd be my pleasure,
you know."

Shannon chuckled a little and put her arm around my shoulder,
leading me into the living room. "Thanks for wanting to protect me,
Molly, but it's going to be okay."

I simply shrugged my shoulders and sighed.

The warmth of the fireplace set the mood as the four of us sat in
the living room talking, and even laughing about the many aspects
of life we all had in common at the moment. We had just finished
discussing the nightmare of final exams and had moved on to the
amazing experience of having an ultrasound, when the doorbell rang

and the room suddenly went quiet.

I was about to stand up when Gordon placed his hand on my knee. "I'll get it," he said and quickly rose to his feet (something he could do much faster than me these days). I let the weight of my body fall back into the couch since there was nothing else I could do. I'd tried to fight this moment from even happening, but in the end it didn't really matter how I felt. I reminded myself once again that this had nothing to do with me. As a precautionary measure, I folded my arms across my chest to contain the many emotions and aggravations that surely would want to come out the moment Chad Hanks began to speak.

"Hey, there. Here, come on in out of the cold." I was a bit irritated at how cheerful and welcoming Gordon's voice sounded.

I almost hated to even look over toward the door, so I looked at Shannon instead. She was holding onto Justin's hand and I soon noticed that both of their eyes took on a bit of a surprised expression. Then, I looked to the entryway and realized why.

As expected, Chad Hanks, with his athletic stature and good looks was standing in the entry way of my parent's house. But next to him stood a petite, dark haired woman holding a small bundle in her arms.

Justin and Shannon were soon on their feet, so I decided I'd better join them. The previous warmth I'd been feeling had been quickly replaced with a sense of awkwardness. Gordon soon attempted to remedy the situation.

"How ya doin'?" he said, shaking hands with Chad.

"Just fine," he replied, and then turned to the woman at his side. "This is my wife Maria and our son Jordan. He's five weeks old today."

Chapter
TWENTY

When Chad Hanks entered my parent's house with a wife and baby, I was forced to excavate every minute particle of self-control buried within my entire being to keep from shouting, *"No way!"* But somehow I managed to rein in those emotions to a mere expression of bewilderment. Actually, I think we were all a bit dumbfounded, even Gordon.

Within fifteen seconds, however, I was convinced that my husband would make a great diplomat the way he took charge of a somewhat awkward situation for all involved.

"Congratulations," said Gordon as he slapped Chad on the back. "I didn't even realize you were married. And look at this little guy." Gordon motioned toward the baby.

Chad looked a bit uncomfortable as he spoke. "Well, actually, we were just married last week—a small ceremony at Maria's parents' house in Twin Falls."

Gordon didn't miss a beat. "Well, like I said, congratulations."

At this point, I guess Gordon realized that the rest of us were still standing back a bit so he proceeded to do some introductions, which were painfully unnecessary for some of us. I almost felt sorry for my husband as he attempted to make everyone in the room feel a bit more comfortable—not an easy job under the circumstances. The guy deserved the Nobel peace prize, or at least a big hug or a twenty minute foot massage when this was all over.

"Maria, this is my wife, Molly, and her cousin, Shannon." Gordon directed his hand toward me and then Shannon. "And this is Shannon's husband, Justin. Justin, this is Chad Hanks."

I almost held my breath as the two men approached each other. Maybe I'd seen one too many Hollywood movies, but a part of me wondered if instead of shaking hands, they might start swinging fists. But the two men stood face-to-face and calmly extended their hands.

Although Chad had the stockier build of the two, their similarities were freakishly eerie. They were both tall in stature with golden-blond hair and blue eyes—your basic, all-American good looks.

When the men stepped back, Chad turned his attention to my cousin.

"Hello, Shannon."

Shannon, who looked rather calm considering the turmoil I knew she must be feeling, simply gave Chad a nod and a brief acknowledgement.

"Hello."

She was the epitome of composure—truly amazing. If I had been in my cousin's shoes, I'm sure a few other words besides 'hello' might have crossed my lips by this point.

I had to wonder if my thoughts were reflected in my expression or body language, because when I glanced over to Gordon, he was giving me one of those "I hope you behave" type of looks. I mean, really, did I look like some sort of playground bully, ready to pick a fight?

I turned my eyes back to my ever-perceptive husband, giving him my best "you don't have to remind me to act civil" expression. Then, I plastered a smile onto my face and interlocked my fingers together in front of me to offset any sudden urge I might develop to punch Chad Hanks in the nose.

"Here, let me take your coats and then we can all sit in the living room." Chad helped Maria off with her coat as she carefully juggled the baby, and I couldn't help but wonder when the guy became so thoughtful.

When we were all seated, I expected Gordon to take up where he'd left off with his diplomatic efforts. It was Chad, however, who spoke first. His voice was shaky. The guy was obviously nervous, but I had to give him credit, he sure was determined.

"Hey, I know it's Christmas Eve, and you have better things to do tonight than sit here and chat with me, so I'll try to make this brief.

"First of all, I wanted to thank you, Shannon and Justin, for agreeing to talk with me tonight. You had every reason, every reason in the world, to tell me to get lost. And if, if that had been your decision, well, then, I would have understood. Completely understood."

As Chad searched for the right words, I couldn't help but notice Maria reach over to her husband, giving his knee a reassuring squeeze. His muscular chest rose and then fell as he took a deep breath to compose himself.

Chad looked down at his hands and then cleared his throat before continuing. "I've made a lot of mistakes in my life and hurt a few people along the way. I'm not proud of that." He raised his eyes to focus in on my cousin.

"Shannon, I was such a jerk back in high school—a complete fool. But a lot of things have changed in my life." Chad placed his hand over Maria's.

"I've wanted to call you so many times to tell you how sorry I am for what I caused you to go through—alone."

Chad combed his fingers through his hair. His eyes shifted down again, and he shook his head back and forth ever so slightly. "I just couldn't bring myself to do it, to talk to you."

I looked over at Shannon to see what her reaction was to all of this, and I was a little surprised to see my cousin's red and glistening eyes attempting to blink back tears. Somehow I'd thought that she'd be angry. No, I'd thought she'd be furious. Didn't she deserve to throw a tantrum or something? Or at least yell at the guy a little. Wouldn't that make her feel better?

But there she sat with Justin's arm around her, looking sad, yet secure and even serene. This was *not* the reaction I expected.

Aside from the crackling of wood in the large, stone fireplace, the room seemed to be frozen in silence. It was rekindled, however, when Chad reached one free hand over to the infant in his wife's arms and brushed the back of his large finger against the delicate skin of the sleeping baby's cheek.

"I never realized how much parents love their children until this little guy came around." Chad almost started to smile, but then his countenance turned serious as he looked back into Shannon's face. A single tear began to trickle down his cheek, but he quickly wiped it away.

"I heard that we, I mean, I heard that the baby was a little girl."

I had to strain to hear, as Shannon's voice was only a whisper. "She was beautiful. So beautiful."

Chad lowered his head as his shoulders began to shake first in little vibrations that quickly grew into jagged shuddering.

"I'm so sorry, Shannon, so sorry!"

Maria, whose eyes were also full of tears, put her free arm around her husband's back and leaned her head into his strong shoulder.

After Chad gained some composure, he attempted to speak again. "I don't expect you to forgive me—I don't deserve your forgiveness— but you have to know that I'm truly sorry for everything that happened and that you had to go through it all alone. I know I wasn't ready to be a father back then, but at least I could have been a friend."

Once again, I was taken by surprise when Shannon stood up and walked over to Chad, knelt down in front of him and took hold of his hand. Through wet eyes, my cousin wore an expression of understanding and serenity. The moment she spoke, I knew why.

"I forgave you a long time ago."

"But I don't understand. I never even spoke to you during that whole time, or since." Chad's eyebrows were furrowed in bewilderment. No doubt mine were doing the same thing. I turned my head to read Gordon's expression, but he was simply wearing a smile.

"I had to forgive you, Chad, and forgive myself," Shannon replied. "I needed to get on with my life, and I have, with a little help." Shannon turned her head to Justin and smiled. Then she stood up and placed her hand on the round part of her stomach.

"And you're not the only one getting a second chance." A grin surfaced on Shannon's face, lightening the mood.

Chad chuckled a bit as he blinked his eyes a few times and then turned to Justin.

"You have an amazing wife," he said.

"Looks like we both do," Justin replied.

Chad put his arm back around his wife, while Shannon sidestepped back to the couch and Justin.

The conversation quickly shifted to a more comfortable subject— the previous ISU football season—but to be honest, I didn't hear a word of what was being said. I was still lost in the previous conversation as it played repeatedly in my head. And every time I looked over at Shannon to see if she was okay, I was shocked and amazed at the tranquility radiating from within her.

At that moment, I was forced to reflect upon my own hostile feelings toward Chad Hanks. I had always defended my malicious thoughts toward him as some sort of allegiance to my cousin. It had always seemed like a good enough excuse, but with Shannon's revelation that she'd forgiven him long ago, enabling her to move forward with her life, I had to wonder why *I* was still holding a grudge. The only purpose it seemed to serve was to fuel even more anger within me. Anger which I knew couldn't be attractive to Gordon. And anger which, undoubtedly, prevented me from all the blessings of the Spirit. No wonder I seemed to be in such a heap of trouble these days with so many people.

Before long, everyone left, and Gordon and I were heading up to bed. I felt totally drained of any energy. I suppose I could have blamed my exhaustion on the pregnancy—and, actually, it probably was a contributing factor. But another part of me was simply tired from my own little man-made messes—or should I say, Molly-made messes.

"You feeling okay?" Gordon said as we reached the top of the stairs. "You've been kind of quiet the last hour or so."

"I'll be fine. I think I just need a good night's sleep."

"Yeah, I suppose we'd better get to bed before Santa Claus arrives."

In all the activity of the last few hours, I'd almost forgotten it was Christmas Eve. A spark of excitement flickered in my heart. I'd always loved Christmas, and being here at my parent's house with Gordon, and the knowledge that I was carrying twins, would undoubtedly, make this the best Christmas I'd experienced in all of my twenty-one years.

As we were about to reach my bedroom door, I turned around to face my husband. "So what do you hope Santa brings you for Christmas this year?"

Gordon slowly placed his arms around my ever increasing waistline and pulled me in close, well, as close as my belly would allow. His voice was soft, and his eyes sincere. "To be honest, I have everything in the world that I've ever wanted right here in my arms. Just give me eternity, and I'm set."

"It's yours," I replied as our lips met.

The sweetness of the moment was cut short, however, when my little brother, Dusty, bounded out of the bathroom and into our little public display of affection. Immediately, he threw up his arm to shield us from his vision.

"Oh, please!"

Chapter
TWENTY-ONE

For some reason I woke with a start on Christmas morning. As I looked at the sheer curtains covering the window, I could tell that the day was overcast—a perfect excuse to pull the covers up to my ears and fall back asleep. But, it was Christmas morning, sleeping in wasn't an option. When I rolled over toward Gordon, I was surprised to see him staring back at me.

"How long have you been awake?" I asked.

"Just a little while—I've been thinking." Gordon snuggled up next to me, and as usual, placed one of his hands on my belly.

"What ya thinking about?"

"You," he replied, and kissed the top of my head.

Pulling in closer to Gordon, I rested my head on his chest. I couldn't help but wonder how life could possibly get any better than at this very moment.

Gordon continued, "Actually, I was wondering what it would be like if we had to put you on a donkey and travel up to Burley."

"What?"

"You know, like Mary and Joseph."

I placed my hand on top of Gordon's hand, which was still resting on my belly, and thought for a moment of what that long-ago trip to Bethlehem might have been like—a sobering thought.

"I'm only halfway through this pregnancy and I can tell you right now, as much as I love my horse, I won't be riding him, or a donkey, any time soon. And if I had to give birth in a stable, well . . ." I couldn't even finish my thought because it was truly unimaginable. And yet, these were the humble circumstances that the Savior of the world was born into.

Gordon spoke quietly into my ear, "Hard to even imagine, isn't it?"

"Incredibly hard, and yet I have no doubt that it happened—that the Savior was born, lived, and died for us. How else could Shannon sit there, face-to-face with the guy who practically destroyed her teenage years (as well as nearly scarring the rest of her life) and yet look so peaceful—so forgiving?"

Gordon didn't say anything, just listened as I continued to express the thoughts that had been weighing heavily on my mind since the events of the previous night.

"You know, Gordon, I thought I understood the atonement, I really did. But until last night, I'm not sure I'd ever really seen first-hand the magnitude of its healing power. I'd always associated it with seeking repentance, but I don't know that I'd ever really applied it to forgiving those who have wronged us. I learned last night that the two go hand in hand. Shannon somehow knew this a long time ago. The girl is amazing."

"Ya know, you're pretty amazing yourself," said Gordon.

"Yeah, right, about as amazing as Silly Putty."

Gordon's voice grew serious. "Hey, now, don't knock 'The Putty.' That stuff gave me hours of entertainment in my youth. Did you know it can bounce like a ball? And if you flatten it out over a comic strip," my husband began to press the palms of his hands together, "and then pull it up, the image of the comic will be imprinted on it. And then you can stretch it out and—" Gordon suddenly stopped talking, his hands frozen in a pulling motion as he began sniffing.

"You catching a cold or something?"

"No, I'm catching a whiff of bacon." Somehow I wasn't at all surprised that smells coming from my mom's kitchen would totally sidetrack Gordon. This only reinforced my notion that the guy was part bloodhound or something.

"I think that's Mom's subtle cue for all of us to get out of bed."

Gordon's eyes widened. "I like the way your mom does things."

I rolled up my pillow into a ball and propped it under my arm. "I have to admit, I didn't always appreciate her ways growing up. But now I realize just how incredible she was—and is." I briefly looked down at my stomach. "I only hope I can be half the mother she is."

Gordon scooted up on one elbow so we could be face to face as he spoke. "I meant what I said earlier. You *are* amazing. And I just know that our kids are going to be as crazy about you as you are about your mom."

Half-way through Gordon's sincere remarks, I threw my hand over my mouth and began to laugh.

"What's so funny?" said Gordon.

I wiped at the moisture coming from my eyes with the back of my hand before speaking. "For a moment there I thought you were going to say that our kids were going to be as crazy as me."

Gordon's voice, as well as facial expression, was completely serious. "Oh, well, of course. I thought that was a given."

"What?!" That was it. I'd had about enough so I reached under my arm, pulled out my fluffy down pillow and proceeded to wallop my husband right on top of his head.

A fifteen minute, all-out pillow fight ensued. Who said that fighting wasn't a good thing?

Christmas morning at the Chamber's house had changed a bit over the years. When my brother's and I were little, we were up way before the sun, rummaging through our stockings in search of a pre-breakfast snack of candy canes and chocolate-covered, marshmallow-filled Santas. These treats from the North Pole were certain to have our bellies aching by breakfast, but who could worry about such a minor inconvenience on this, the most magical day of the year.

After the initial raid of the stockings, my older brothers and I took great pleasure in sorting and stacking the various gifts for each family member, always with the secret hope that we'd be the lucky one that year with the largest stack. I know Mom did her best to keep things even, and the number of gifts was generally the same, but as children, size ruled. Since baby dolls and Barbies are larger than action figures and match box cars, I was often the one with the largest stack. I think my brothers thought it was a conspiracy. I just figured it was payback for having to put up with their stinky socks and obnoxious knock-knock jokes the previous eleven months.

This Christmas morning was different. First, we sat down to a delicious breakfast where the conversation revolved around the happenings of our lives. Our various gifts sat unsorted and untouched under the Christmas tree—hopefully a sign of maturity on all accounts.

Even Curt was talkative again—a sure sign that he was in better spirits. Apparently he'd talked to Amy for quite a while the previous night. But, all he'd say about it was, "It went well." I could only hope.

Before too long, we were all drawn to the living room to open gifts. And even though our family now consisted mostly of adults, there was still that sense of excitement buzzing through the air. For me, it mostly revolved around the special surprise Gordon and I had planned for my parents.

One by one, presents were opened and "oohs" and "aahs" were shared, while trash bags of crumpled wrapping paper and discarded boxes were collected. It was quite a contrast from the free-for-all gift opening rampage of our earlier days.

Everyone seemed pleased with my homemade gifts (either that or they were all great liars). And even though it was probably seventy-five degrees in the living room with the fireplace crackling hot, Gordon insisted on wearing the grey scarf that I'd managed to crochet while he was working evenings at the grocery store.

As the gift giving began to wind down, Gordon magically pro-duced a medium-sized box. "Hey, what do we have here?" he said, sounding surprised at his own little trick. I figured he'd been hiding a gift for me, but with our budget, I wasn't expecting much—and that was okay. Fancy perfume and jewelry would have to wait. For the time being, I could make do with nice smelling deodorant and my CTR ring.

Gordon placed the box on my lap, and I did what all curious kids do—I shook it. "Hmmmm, it's definitely not solid." I looked over at Gordon, but all he'd do was shrug.

Without further delay, I ripped off the wrapping paper to expose a box of fudge covered Oreos. "These are my favorites!" I squealed.

Just as I was about to throw my arms around my husband, I no-ticed that the plastic wrapping around the box had been carefully cut around the three sides, and then taped back in to place.

I looked at Gordon. "Did you eat some of my fudge-covered Oreos?"

Once again, Gordon shrugged. "A guy gets hungry."

I peeled off one of the strips of tape with my fingernail and then proceeded to pull the rest of the plastic cover from the white cookie box. As I opened the lid, I was surprised (and to be honest, pleased) to see only one cookie missing. In its place sat a little black velvet bag pulled tight at the top with strings. Only one thought occurred to me—CTR rings *don't* come in little black velvet bags.

Aside from the jabbering of my little niece, Alexi, as she played with her new doll, the room was quiet as I loosened the strings of the bag, reached in, and pulled out a long silver chain holding a silver rectangular charm.

"It says something," said Curt who was sitting on the other side of me.

As I held up the chain and placed the rectangular piece in the palm of my hand, I read the engraving, "Alma 56:47." To be honest, I had no clue what that particular scripture was, but knowing my husband and how he "collected" scriptures, I knew it must be something significant.

Gordon took the chain from my hand and placed it over my head and around my neck as he recited from memory the words to the scripture: *"They had been taught by their mothers that if they did not doubt, God would deliver them."*

"The stripling warriors!" I nearly cheered as I examined the pristine silver surface. "But how could we afford this?"

Gordon ignored my question as he took my hand, placed the charm inside of it, and wrapped his larger hand around mine.

"I want you to do a favor for me, Molly."

I just nodded my head, because I knew if I spoke, the tears would take over.

"Any time you ever start to doubt your capabilities, or importance, as a mother, I want you to look at this little charm, and recite this scripture."

I was still in a little bit of shock as Gordon leaned in and gave me a kiss. A round of "aahs" surfaced, and when I looked over at the others in the room, Mom and Tiffany (my sister-in-law), were both in tears, while the guys just looked restless. Go figure. Dusty was even starting to head out of the room.

"Wait," I nearly yelled, as I wiped at my eyes. There's one last gift. And even though it's for everyone—especially me and Gordon—we'd like Mom and Dad to do the honors."

I pulled a flat rectangular shaped gift from behind a pillow at my side, handed it to Gordon, who stood and handed it to my mom.

Mom looked at me with raised eyebrows, while Dad gently nudged her with his elbow. "Well, let's open this thing and see what the fuss is all about."

"Be patient, Norm," Mom scolded, as she slid one finger under the fold in the wrapping paper and carefully slid it to loosen the tape. After what seemed like an eternity to the rest of us wrapping paper "rippers," Mom carefully folded back the paper (which she would never use again, by the way) to reveal one of my hand-painted picture frames. But, as she tilted her head to get a better glance at the picture, she looked somewhat perplexed.

Without saying anything, Mom handed it to Dad who squinted his eyes, cocked his head, and even turned the frame upside down."

"What the heck are you two looking at?" Dusty finally asked.

Dad's voice matched his expression. "Gray fuzz?"

"It's an ultrasound picture," said Mom, "but what does it mean?"

All eyes were now focused on me. After standing up from where I was sitting next to Gordon, I walked over to Mom and Dad and proceeded to squeeze into the love seat between them.

When I'd finally managed to wedge my ever widening rear end between my parents, I pointed to a spot on the "gray fuzz."

"See that?"

"Uh-huh," they said in unison.

"That's a head, our baby's head." Mom took on an expression of total wonderment. Dad still look confused, but I continued my speech anyway. "And the ultrasound technician said it's a boy."

Cheers went up in the entire room with the news that I'd be providing the Chambers family with their first grandson. I waited for a moment until the noise began to subside. "And see this here?"

"Yeah," said Mom.

"That's a head, too."

"Two *heads?*" Dusty nearly shouted.

"Two babies," I clarified. "We're having twins."

Chapter
TWENTY-TWO

The remainder of our semester break was actually quite lonely at times. Gordon was working long days at the grocery store and Curt was still in Oakley helping Uncle Paul and Aunt Reita with some remodeling work on their house. My only consolation was that Amy had arrived back from Tulsa. Unfortunately, she was staying busy with the women's basketball team. The season was well under way. I loved it when Amy was around, but often she was on the road.

I decided to take advantage of this time by catching up on "fun" reading. All semester long it seemed like my reading choices were dictated by professors who had nothing better to do than dole out volumes of textbook reading assignments that were generally about as fascinating as your basic VCR manual. But after a quick trip to the library, I came home armed with such titles as *Ready or Not . . . Here We Come!*, *Mothering Multiples*, and *Baby 411*, as well as a few light romances (I definitely needed that little diversion).

And thus commenced my pre-semester reading binge: I read in bed, I read on the couch, I even read in the bathroom (use your imagination). My favorite reading attire was anything loose—often my pajamas. And why not? Pajamas are comfortable. And mine were even cute, in a flannel sort of way. At some point (usually a half hour before Gordon was expected home) I did try to shower and be in actual clothes—those things people wear when they're not in hibernation and someone might actually see them at some point during the day.

I called these two weeks, "Babies 101" and refused to feel any sort of guilt for this indulgence. How else was I supposed to learn about such things as nursing strikes, teething rings, rice cereal, and rectal thermometers—apparently we'd be needing one soon.

But just as any other good thing, my two weeks of hibernation had to come to an end. Before I knew what was happening, Curt was back from Oakley, Gordon was working nights at the grocery store, and the spring semester at Idaho State University was underway.

"I can't believe you're taking classes this semester," said Amy as we sat at a table in the cafeteria. "Are you crazy?"

I rolled my eyes and took a deep breath before reciting my standard reply. "Maybe I am, but it's sure not going to get any easier once the babies are here. Besides, I'm not due till the third week in May and finals are the second week. I'll have a whole week to spare."

"You're a lunatic," Amy reiterated.

"Thanks, I appreciate your vote of confidence."

"I mean that in the most loving way, Molly."

"Sure you do," I replied, picking up one of Amy's long french fries and guiltlessly shoving it into my mouth.

Amy smiled and slowly shook her head. "You're just like your brother."

"Well, since I'm older than Curt, that would make *him* just like *me*! And speaking of which, what's going on with you two anyway? I thought when you talked on Christmas Eve you worked everything out."

Amy tilted her head to one side. "Is that what he told you?"

"Not exactly. I just kind of assumed—"

Amy put her one hand up. "Look, it's no big mystery or secret. I simply agreed to learn a little about your church. Hopefully to gain some insight into just why guys like Curt and Gordon are willing to spend all of their hard-earned savings and two prime years that any sane person would devote to their college education, to become preachers."

"Missionaries," I corrected.

"Missionaries . . . preachers . . . saints . . . whatever," Amy replied. "And I have to tell you: the only thing I like about this whole mission idea is that Curt said they're not allowed to date. Seems to me, that fact alone would scare most guys from even thinking about going, but not your brother."

"Oh, it'll be a sacrifice for Curt, all of it is. Especially, leaving you behind. But, he wouldn't be willing to do it if it wasn't so important."

"I guess that's what I want to know. Why is it so important?"

While Amy was talking, I found myself fingering the silver necklace Gordon had given me for Christmas. As my fingertips wandered down the chain to the flat silver surface of the charm, I looked at the inscription and subconsciously read it out loud.

"Alma 56:47."

Amy's expression was blank. "Is that some sort of locker combination?"

My eyes were still focused on the engraving. "The stripling warriors."

Amy raised an eyebrow. "Excuse me?"

"Gordon and Curt, they're like the stripling warriors in the Book of Mormon; willing to sacrifice everything—or at least two very important years of their life—because of their great faith. '*They had been taught by their mothers that if they did not doubt, God would deliver them.*'"

Amy picked up a french fry and pointed it at me, while raising an eyebrow. "So, you're telling me that God wants Curt to go on this mission. And that if he does, he'll be saved or something?"

I took a deep breath and slowly let it out. This wasn't going how I hoped it would. Suddenly, a thought occurred to me. "Have you ever met a missionary before?"

"A Mormon missionary? The guys on the bikes?"

"Yeah. You know, dark suits, name tags."

"Well, to be honest, up until this point, I've pretty much tried to avoid them."

"Why? Gordon was one. He's harmless."

"That's a matter of perspective." Amy tried to hold a straight face as she spoke, but when I nearly choked on my apple juice, we both lost it and began to laugh.

Amy threw her hands up in resignation. "Oh, alright. Bring on your Mormon preachers. How much more frightening could they be than you, Curt, Gordon, and your stories of naked warriors!"

"Strip*ling . . . la, la, la, ling*—not *stripping!*"

Amy simply laughed.

❈❈❈

It's one thing for someone to say that they'll meet with the missionaries. It's a whole other story to actually nail down a date, time, and place. At least twice I'd made arrangements for the much anticipated meeting only to have it fall through, and always on my dear friend Amy's account. Whether it was an unexpected change in her basketball schedule, or too much homework, the fact remained that she still hadn't followed through with this meeting.

After analyzing the situation, I decided that a certain key element was missing from the equation; my secret weapon, so to speak—food! If I knew Amy, all it would take was a pan of cheese-laden lasagna and a loaf of buttery french bread, and the girl would be a captive audience for a good half hour (forty-five minutes if I threw in blueberry cheesecake). Gordon shook his head at my plan, Curt patted his stomach, and I simply held my head high and proceeded with the preparations.

When the evening of the meal/meeting with the missionaries finally arrived, Amy showed up right on time, no doubt to enjoy a warm dinner. I could only hope that she'd warm up to the missionaries as well.

As Amy descended the stairs into our basement apartment, I half expected her to turn tail and run the minute she encountered the missionaries. But, I must admit, she surprised me with her calm demeanor and friendly disposition.

"Amy, I'd like you to meet Sister Barton and Sister Tyler," I motioned my hand toward each sister as I made the introductions. "They're both serving full-time missions for our church, and they're joining us for dinner tonight."

"Nice to meet you," Amy responded quite cordially, and I was greatly relieved. I really didn't think she'd do something horrendous or embarrassing, I was just a little wary of my friend's subtle interrogation tactics (for lack of a better description).

I suppose, however, I should have been more concerned about what would transpire between Amy and Curt. The tension between the two was not only visible but also tangible. Once again, I had to wonder what I'd gotten myself into, but when I looked again toward the missionaries and felt their genuine spirit of love, I knew this was all happening for a purpose and reason.

When we were all seated around the table enjoying the gooey lasagna, Amy was the first to speak.

"I didn't realize your church had female missionaries. I like that."

"I do too," said Sister Tyler. She was probably as tall as Amy, and had long blond hair pulled back into a ponytail.

Amy smiled innocently at the sister missionaries and then dove in with her first question. I could only hope the sisters could swim.

"So, why exactly did you decide to go on a mission, if you don't mind my asking?"

Sister Tyler's face became almost animated. "I've always wanted to serve a mission, ever since I was a little girl. But, I guess, the dream became a true commitment and goal when I was fourteen and saw one of my favorite cousins serve a mission. We wrote letters the whole time she was gone, and I just knew that I wanted this experience for myself."

Amy smiled. "I guess I can understand that. I know what it's like to have a dream, a goal. I've wanted to play basketball my entire life. In fifth grade I used to shoot hoops with the boys during recess—broke all sorts of playground 'social rules,' but I didn't care. It had always been my dream. What good are we if we can't follow our dreams." Amy turned her gaze to Curt.

"So, Curt, have you always wanted to serve a mission your entire life? Is this your boyhood dream?"

Curt had just inserted a fork-full of lasagna into his mouth, and from the half-gagging expression that suddenly distorted his face, it looked like he'd swallowed a lump of cheese before chewing.

After recovering, Curt finally replied, "Uh, yeah, I guess. Sure."

Amy didn't look convinced, but Gordon quickly jumped into the conversation. "I think most boys that grow up in the Church at some point or another question if they really want to serve a mission. It's only natural when dealing with such a major decision. I wasn't raised in the church, but I recognized immediately something special in the missionaries that taught me the gospel. I wanted to be just like them, to have that same peace. When I was baptized at the age of sixteen, I knew that someday I'd be a missionary."

Dinner continued on as the conversation strayed to various aspects of missionary work, with both sister missionaries essentially bearing their testimonies to the blessings they've received while serving a mission. I couldn't help but notice, however, how quiet my brother remained the entire evening—not a great sign.

After dinner we moved into the living room where the sisters shared a brief lesson that included such aspects as the apostasy, the restoration, Joseph Smith, and even eternal families. The spirit was very strong, and by evaluating Amy's reactions and comments, it seemed that she was quite interested. Of course, I could never be sure of anything with my dear friend.

All good things must come to an end, however. This evening was no exception. It wasn't long before Amy announced that she still had a ton of homework waiting back at the dorm for her. I was a little surprised when Curt offered to drive Amy home and she accepted. Aside from the brief exchange during dinner, the two had hardly spoken to each other.

When the guests left, and the apartment was finally quiet, Gordon and I stood side by side at the kitchen sink washing dishes. It had been a long evening physically, and emotionally, so I briefly rested my head on Gordon's shoulder.

"I'm worried about Curt. I think he's questioning his decision to serve a mission."

Gordon lifted a soggy hand out of the water and gave it a little shake before placing it around my shoulder.

"Maybe that's a good thing."

I stopped washing and turned to face Gordon. "But I don't want him having doubts."

"Molly, your brother needs to sort through his feelings *before* he goes out into the mission field. Do you have any idea how many guys don't make it past the Missionary Training Center?"

"What do you mean?" I asked.

"Way too many guys get all the way to the MTC and then start questioning their decision, and end up calling their parents and going home. I saw it more than once. It's a bad deal all around."

"So what can I do?" I asked.

"This isn't something you can fix for your brother."

For once I was at a loss for words and the frustration seemed overwhelming. I was used to stepping in and trying to help in so many situations—especially involving people I loved. But, I knew Gordon's words were true.

I leaned my head onto my husband's shoulder and he pulled me close, whispering in my ear, "There *is* one thing you can do for your brother."

I quickly pulled my head back, searching Gordon's face for some good news. "What?"

"You can pray for him."

I let my head fall back onto Gordon's shoulder, absorbing his words. *Yes, I can pray for him.*

Chapter
TWENTY-THREE

Saturday to college students is like Chap Stick to your average set of lips; they benefit tremendously from the therapeutic relief and healing it provides—especially during the winter months when they're about to crack!

It was Gordon's day off from the grocery store, but he had lab work to catch up on, so he headed out early in the morning to the engineering building before I even woke up. I, on the other hand, had absolutely no intention of even glancing at a textbook for the next forty-eight hours. I had worked hard all week to get my homework done, and the only things I planned to read over the weekend could either be found on the back of a cereal box or on the New York Times bestseller list. (Okay, and maybe the comics from the Sunday newspaper).

As I was dubiously checking out the box of frosted shredded wheat abandoned on the kitchen table by either Gordon or Curt, a better idea for a morning meal seized my mind and appetite. I was going to make waffles—real, made-from-scratch, honest-to-goodness waffles whose square crevasses would accommodate pools of thick, rich, maple syrup that would make any dieter toss out their melba toast and scramble for the nearest fork.

After unearthing the brand-new waffle iron from a stack of un-opened wedding gifts hiding under our bed, I headed back to the kitchen, ready to create a culinary masterpiece. The recipe was fairly straightforward, so within a matter of minutes—okay, a half hour—my first golden-crisp waffle was ready for consumption. But, since I had at least a quart of batter left, I decided to cook it all up so we could reheat waffles in the microwave for a delicious, no-fuss, Sunday breakfast.

Just as I was pulling the last waffle from the waffle iron, Curt entered the kitchen with one of those lost puppy dog looks on his face.

"You hungry?" I asked holding up the plate stacked high with steaming waffles.

"You're killing me, Molly."

"What? What did I do?"

Curt placed his hands on his stomach. "I'm fasting today, and you go and make waffles for breakfast."

"I'm sorry, I didn't know you were fasting. What's the occasion?"

"I just need some clarity on a few things, that's all."

I hated to pry, but my curiosity got the best of me. "Like whether to serve a mission?"

"No, more like *why*."

"What do you mean?" I asked.

"I need to know for sure that I've made this decision to go on a mission for the right reasons." Curt lifted up the edge of the waffle plate with his finger, put it back down, and then turned to face the cupboards. "Am I doing it because Mom and Dad want me to? Or because Dad, and Alex, and Blake went, and now it's my turn? Am I doing it just to prove to Amy that I have goals and dreams too? Or am I doing it because I know deep in my heart that it's the right thing to do—it's Heavenly Father's plan for me?"

I wanted to shout out, *Yes, yes, that's it!* But I didn't.

"Is there anything I can do for you?" I finally asked.

"Actually, yeah." Curt's hand went to his stomach before speaking. "For lunch, make yourself something to eat that doesn't smell quite so good. Matter of fact, make something that doesn't smell *at all*, like peanut butter and jelly."

When Gordon arrived home that Saturday afternoon, I was more than ready to head over to the Reed Gym to take in the Lady Bengals basketball game against Weber State. Amy had been playing well all season and I was fairly certain the coach would put her in as a two-guard at some point in this afternoon's game. Not only was she a great shooter, she played excellent defense as well. The only thing holding her back this season was her status as a freshman player— something she had no control over. In the end, however, talent almost always prevailed over seniority.

As we entered the gym and began to absorb the excitement and energy. I must admit I felt a smidgen of envy toward Amy and the rest of my former teammates. I'd hoped these feelings would pass, but each time I attended a game, a small part inside felt as if it had been abandoned. I could only hope that the babies would somehow fill this void. Either that, or create a new sense of fulfillment. In a way, I think this was already happening.

After the game was finally underway, my sense of longing to play competitive basketball was soon replaced with a more intense desire for my friends and former teammates to do their best, to win. I was content to be their biggest fan (and the way my stomach was growing, I soon would be).

"Go Bengals! Woooh!" I hollered with one hand cupped to my mouth, while the other was placed instinctively over my bulging belly like your average pregnant basketball fanatic.

Gordon leaned over toward me, speaking loud enough so I could hear over the pandemonium of the crowd. "Aren't you worried you'll scare the babies by yelling so loud?"

I waved off Gordon's concern with my hand. "Oh, don't worry. They'll need to get used to it sooner or later." I really tried to keep a straight face, but when I looked into Gordon's stunned expression, I could tell the guy thought I was serious. "I'm kidding, I'm kidding! Besides, I only yell on roller coasters and at basketball games."

Good 'ol Curt, eavesdropping on our conversation, couldn't help but chime in. "Yeah, right. And she only cries during sad movies and only eats when she's hungry."

I gave Curt my best evil eye, but it only served to amuse that twerpy, not-so-little brother of mine.

Curt turned to Gordon and held up the three fingers of his right hand like any good scout. "I speak the truth. Trust me. You've only been living with her for less than a year. I've been with her a lifetime."

"We can change that, you know? Just say the word and I'm sure we can find you a nice little dorm room somewhere." I gave my brother the best scowl my eyebrows could manage before my expression softened into a grin.

"Hey, look," Gordon hollered. "The coach is putting Amy in."

I began to yell again in support of my friend, and this time Curt and Gordon joined in. The game against Weber State had started off quite intense and continued at that level with the score escalating at a somewhat even rate, basket for basket. The Lady Bengals were holding strong. I was very proud of my team.

Amy looked great handling the ball. She was a natural athlete who moved with ease up and down the court. Generally, she would pass the ball off to Becka or Jill, but several times she found an opening, allowing her to shoot. Once she even made a three pointer. The crowd loved that!

With only a minute before halftime, Amy was once again in control of the ball, but she was having a heck of a time. A tall redhead from the other team was right on top of her as Amy shifted her weight back and forth in an attempt to break free. Finally, in a bold move, Amy pivoted to the left at the same moment the redhead rushed forward, knocking Amy down onto the court. A foul was called.

The crowd began to boo at the aggressive actions of the redhead and I was about to join in, when I realized that, after several seconds, Amy was still lying on the court. She had turned on her side and rolled into a ball with both hands cupped over her left kneecap.

"What's going on?" Curt yelled to no one in particular. An ominous feeling settled over me, and all I could do was hold my hands over my mouth—maybe to keep from screaming, although I don't think any sound would have been able to come out. I felt hollow inside and barely noticed Gordon's arm slide around my shoulder.

Curt left the spot next to me and Gordon and hastily made his way down the bleachers and out onto the court where the coach, a few players, and some emergency medical personnel were gathered around Amy. With all the bodies standing around, we couldn't see anything and it was hard to tell just what was happening. The gravity of the situation became quite clear, however, the moment a stretcher was carried out onto the court.

I was finally able to find my voice. "This isn't good."

"Come on," said Gordon, taking my hand. "Let's find out what's going on."

By the time we made it down to the courtside, Amy was being carried off the court on the stretcher and Curt was walking back toward us.

"Where are they taking her?" I asked.

"Bannock Regional," Curt replied, and nothing more was said as the three of us made our way out of the gym.

When we arrived at the emergency room, we had to wait a good half hour before we were even allowed to see Amy. Finally, a nurse led us to an area curtained off where Amy was laying on a hospital bed. Jean, one of the team trainers was adjusting an ice pack on Amy's knee.

"What the heck happened?" I said as I approached my friend and gently gave her a hug. Her eyes were red and puffy and she looked exhausted.

"I blew out my knee somehow. It hurts to put any weight on it." Moisture began to pool in Amy's eyes. "This is probably going to take me out for the season."

I looked over to Jean for more input on the situation.

"I've seen this before," said Jean. "I'd bet anything it's a torn ACL."

"What does that mean?" I asked, referring to the three letters.

"Surgery." I was surprised to hear Curt reply. "Matt Adams tore his ACL in wrestling last year and had to have surgery."

I looked to Jean with hope in my heart that she would have a better prognosis. She didn't.

"ACL stands for anterior cruciate ligament. They're going to be taking her up to X-ray before long to confirm the doctor's speculation. If this is the case, he's right. She'll need surgery." Jean looked over at Amy. "The good news is that the surgery is arthroscopic—only four small incisions. It's much less invasive than standard knee surgery. Makes for an easier recovery as well."

Curt approached the bed so I moved over toward Gordon. Curt took Amy's hand and held it inside both of his hands. "You'll recover from this, you know. You're strong and determined. I don't think there's anything that could keep you off the basketball court for too long."

Amy leaned her head over toward Curt and her shoulders began to tremble as she faced her reality with tears. "Why did this have to happen? I'm so scared."

Curt put his arm around Amy in an attempt to comfort her, but her sobs seemed to be growing stronger. He finally crouched down so he could look into her face.

"Remember when we talked on Christmas Eve and I was telling you about the priesthood?"

Amy simply nodded and wiped at her eyes with the thin hospital blanket.

"Well, if you'd like, Gordon and I can give you a priesthood blessing." Curt looked up and Gordon gave a quick nod of the head.

Amy's expression softened. "You mean like a prayer to help me get better?"

"Yeah, something like that."

"I'd like that," Amy replied.

Gordon took a small metal vial of oil from his key chain and briefly explained to Amy that it was consecrated oil for the use of blessing the sick and afflicted. I hate to say it, but I half expected some cynical remark to escape from Amy's lips. But instead, she was serene and completely focused on the words spoken, first by Gordon as he sealed the anointing, and then by Curt as he humbly offered up a sincere blessing.

A couple of times during the prayer I wanted to check and see if that was really my little brother speaking. The words were profound and full of wisdom. I was deeply touched.

When the blessing was finished, I opened my teary eyes and realized that Curt was also blinking back moisture. The Spirit had been very strong, and it was evident that all in the room had felt it.

The next hour and a half that we spent with Amy in the emergency room managed to pass with a sense of peace. There were no more tears, and between tests, X-rays and more examinations, we even shared a few good laughs.

When all was said and done for the night, Amy left Bannock Regional Medical Center with a brace on her left knee, crutches under her arms, a bottle of pain pills in her hand, and an appointment the following Monday with an orthopedic specialist. I left with a greater love and respect for my little brother, and for the power of the priesthood.

Chapter
TWENTY-FOUR

The good news: the surgery to repair Amy's torn ACL took place the week following the basketball game and was a complete success. With her determination, athletic abilities, and some help from physical therapy, the doctors predicted a complete recovery.

The bad news: the recovery wasn't going to happen over night, not even in a few weeks or months. Amy would be benched for the remainder of the season, but, most likely, could be back on the court the following year. Not exactly what an athlete wants to hear, but it was her reality, nonetheless.

Amy's emotional condition fluctuated between upbeat and disillusioned about her new physical limitations, which was to be expected. Adjusting from a lifetime of activity to a period of major physical limitations definitely wasn't easy. I knew this firsthand. But overall, she remained in fairly good spirits, perhaps because just before the surgery, she had asked for another priesthood blessing, which Curt and Gordon were more than happy to administer.

A week after the surgery it seemed that both Amy and Curt were changed, and in a good way. I welcomed the opportunity to discuss this metamorphosis with my brother over the weekend since he and I were taking off to Oakley for his final bishop and stake president interview before turning in his mission papers. Gordon was scheduled to work all day Saturday, and knowing how antsy I'd be just sitting at home alone, he encouraged me to go with Curt.

"So this is it, huh?" I asked.

Curt briefly glanced at me from behind the steering wheel of Old Blue with a puzzled look on his face. "This is what?"

"You know, the week the stake president turns in your mission papers."

A spark seemed to ignite in Curt's eyes as the corners of his mouth curled up. "Yep. That's the plan."

"Sooooo, how are you feeling about this?" Actually, I had a pretty good idea how Curt was feeling by his ever present grin, but I guess being the stubborn older sister that I am, I wanted to hear it from his own mouth—an absolute confirmation, you could say.

"I'm psyched! Shouldn't I be?"

"Of course, it's just that a couple of weeks ago you were fasting to gain some sort of clarity with all of this. I guess I was a little concerned, as usual. Looks like you got that clarity you were looking for."

Curt's expression turned introspective as if he were remembering something. When he finally spoke, his voice was soft.

"The Spirit speaks in many different ways, even when we think we're listening for something entirely different."

"You've lost me."

"That day in the emergency room, when we gave Amy a blessing. I was really trying to concentrate on what the Lord wanted me to say."

"I could tell. The Spirit was very strong. I'm sure Amy felt it too."

"It was an interesting sensation though, because at the same time I was giving the blessing and concentrating so hard on the words I should say, I also had an overwhelming confirmation that the Lord really did want me to serve a mission. And even more importantly, I knew in my heart that I wanted to. I really am ready."

"Wow, that's very cool. And is Amy handling it all a little better?"

"She seems to be more understanding, no longer argumentative about the whole thing."

"Really?"

"Don't get me wrong, she's not ready to get baptized or anything. She hasn't boarded the train yet, but she's no longer standing on the tracks either. She seems to understand that I'm doing something important, something that I need to do for me."

As I looked at Curt, he seemed to radiate a sense of peace. He truly was ready.

The remainder of our drive to Oakley passed with both enjoyable conversation, and good music. The only thing lacking was some form of sustenance—munchies, to be exact. But, neither of us were concerned, we knew our Mom too well. Whether through the umbilical cord or ultimate microwave leftovers, this incredible woman lived to nourish her offspring.

The minute we arrived in Oakley, Mom, the master of all things edible, commenced pulling a variety of Tupperware containers from the fridge. In our current state of limited brain function, due to a classic case of textbook mind-clutter, we'd almost forgotten that anything edible could actually be produced from a plastic container retrieved from a refrigerator.

"We've got some leftover spaghetti from earlier tonight. There's also corn, salad, and french bread." Mom stood on her tiptoes and reached to the back of the fridge. "Oh, and here's a little barbeque beef for sandwiches. The buns are in the breadbox." Then she bent over, pulling something rectangular from the bottom shelf. "You'll never believe this. Smith's had peaches on sale. Imagine that, peaches in February, and on sale! Of course I had to buy a few dozen to make peach cobbler. Your dad was beyond thrilled."

Now, had such plastic containers been retrieved from our refrigerator back at The Cave in Pocatello, I might be concerned. With our hectic schedules, Gordon, Curt, and I were notorious for unintentionally growing some pretty interesting science projects in the vast collection of plastic containers we'd received as wedding presents. Our intentions in refrigerating these leftovers were good. *Waste not, want not.*

Our problem was remembering that the leftover lasagna or meatloaf was still in there. If it wasn't gone in two days, the containers would most likely be pushed back by the next evening's assortment of beautifully stored leftovers.

It was easy to recognize the source of our leftover problem, too many plastic containers! Something I'd definitely take into consideration the next time I had to purchase a wedding gift.

Before long, Curt and I had our plates loaded down with leftovers, our tastebuds eager to reunite with the comfort food of our childhood. As I headed for the table, Curt headed for the family room, and the widescreen TV.

"Thanks, Mom," Curt said, slightly raising his plate in the air. "I'm gonna go catch the end of the game with Dad and Dusty."

"Don't forget the cobbler," said Mom.

Curt did a quick about-face and kissed Mom on the cheek. "I'll be back during the commercials, and I'm sure Dad and Dusty won't be far behind me."

While sitting across from Mom, savoring every morsel of real mother-cooked food, I had an epiphany. As usual, my thoughts didn't last long confined to my overloaded brain.

"Will my kids love me as much as I love you?"

"Wow! Where'd that come from?" Mom looked a bit shocked and pleased. "You ought to come visit me and eat my leftovers more often."

"I'm being serious. What if they just don't like me that much?" I put a fork full of spaghetti in my mouth and spoke while attempting to chew. "And what if I never learn to cook like this?" I plunged my fork into the mound of spaghetti and began to twist, knowing full well that I'd never be able to shove such a large heap of rotating pasta into my mouth, but the process was almost mesmerizing as my mind rotated around the prospects of motherhood. Eventually, I pulled the fork back out and scooped up some corn.

Mom reached across the table and took hold of my hand. "They're going to love you more than anyone else in the universe. As a matter of fact, these first few years, you'll actually *be* their universe. And you know what? You're going to love them back even more than they love you."

This was all getting a little confusing. "Sounds like a lotta love floating around our little universe."

"Yup." Mom patted my hand and then took a long sip of her herbal tea. When she set the cup down her eyes got big. "I know what you need, Molly."

I raised my eyebrows. "Yeah, a nanny for my babies. You applying for the job?"

Mom ignored my feeble attempt at humor. Little did she know, I was serious. "You need an afternoon out. Perhaps some lunch. Then some shopping at the mall. Maybe even a matinee?"

"Is this a prescription, or an invitation?"

"Both," Mom said, a slight smile tweaking the corner of her mouth.

By ten o'clock on Saturday morning, Mom and I were headed

down the backcountry roads that led to Twin Falls. It took nearly an hour to get to the Magic Valley Mall, but time passed by enjoyably as Mom and I discussed, in depth, everything from breastfeeding to Brad Pitt.

After I tried on half the maternity clothes in the mall, and we both smeared yummy smelling creams and lotions from Bath & Body Works on every inch of our exposed skin, the two of us found ourselves wandering to the food court for a little nourishment to keep us going. Our goal was to eventually catch an afternoon matinee where we hoped to collapse in the comfort of the cushioned, movie theatre chairs and lose ourselves for a few hours.

Halfway through lunch, Mom made a hasty escape to the women's restroom, so I continued to nibble away on our mountain of fries, lost in contemplating which movie choice would be the best. I generally preferred a light romantic-comedy, but there was also a drama out that had received great reviews, not to mention seven Academy Award nominations.

Just as I was lifting a rather fat fry-sauce-covered french fry to my mouth, a voice caught my immediate attention. "Molly? Is that you?" The male voice was eerily familiar, and it caused a little déjà vu sensation to travel through my body.

"Brandon. What are you doing here?" I asked, and then immediately wished I hadn't. *Duh, what do most people do at a shopping mall?*

Brandon held up a Foot Locker bag. "New shoes."

I smiled and nodded, mostly because at the moment I really had nothing to say that didn't revolve around breastfeeding, Brad Pitt, and the wonderful lotions from Bath & Body Works. Finally, a coherent thought came to my multi-fragrance impaired mind.

"Want a fry?"

Brandon chuckled. "Only if you have fry sauce to go with it."

As he spoke, numerous dates involving me, Brandon, mountains of fries, and buckets of fry sauce drenched my memory. I lifted my fat, greasy fry higher so Brandon would see the sauce, and instantly a large drop of the mayonnaise and ketchup-blended concoction landed right on my shirt.

"Oops," I said as I scooted my plastic chair back and started dabbing at my progressively rounding belly with a wet napkin that only served to fall apart against the friction of the rubbing motion on my shirt.

"Whoa there," said Brandon, apparently a bit shocked by the extension of my abdomen. "I had no idea you were pregnant."

"With twins," I added.

"Congratulations! Wow. All my friends seem to be diving into parenthood. Did you know Chad Hanks has a new baby boy?"

"Actually, yeah."

"He's asked me to bless the baby next Fast Sunday."

"Really?" I said, my eyes widening at the news. Gordon would be pleased to hear this.

"Yep, surprised me too. But he's changed, and for the better. He's not active in the Church, yet," Brandon smiled and gave me one of his infamous winks, "but apparently he has some diligent home teachers."

"That's great," I replied, and hastily shoved the rest of the fry into my mouth before it started dripping again.

My last comment was followed by silence. Awkward silence. The worst kind of awkward silence that is inevitable when two former sweethearts run into each other unexpectedly at the mall. *Where was my mother?*

Brandon finally broke the silence. "Well, hey, it was nice seeing you again. I've got a few more errands to run here in town, so I'd better get going."

I stood up, and then feeling a bit awkward not knowing if I should give him a hug or what, did what any typical Mormon would do, I stuck out my hand. I STUCK OUT MY HAND. For a handshake!

What a dork.

Brandon, ever the gentleman (and seasoned returned missionary), extended his hand across the small table to reach mine. When they met, there were no butterflies fluttering in my stomach, no mystical tingly sensations spreading to my limbs, no hallelujah chorus singing in my ears. It was just a simple gesture of a friendship between two friends. I was grateful for that.

Brandon turned to walk out the doors leading to the parking lot, but when he was about five yards away, he turned back around and pointed to my stomach."

"Hey, and good luck with the twins."

My hand instinctively traveled to my stomach just in time to feel a swift kick. *No butterfly wing behind that kick, that was for sure.*

Chapter
TWENTY-FIVE

If you ever want time to whiz by, enroll as a full-time student. Life will never again be dull, dreary, monotonous or lack-luster—at least until finals are over and you have a chance to kick back with a bag of Doritos and wonder just where in the heck the previous four months disappeared to. Unfortunately, this much anticipated, orange finger-licking event was still over two months away.

I found it crazy how my professors at ISU seemed to gain some sort of demented pleasure in keeping me so doggone busy, I hardly had time to check my watch, let alone, look at the calendar—and I almost didn't need to. All I had to do was glance down at my ever increasing belly to know that time was passing me by.

There was no disputing the great expansion taking place in my midsection. And if I ever wanted to forget about it, there were two sets of fists, feet, knees, and elbows that weren't about to let me, not to mention a husband that would carry on complete conversations with our unborn children via my belly button—in private, thank goodness.

As I attempted to find some sort of comfortable position on the couch, hoping to get a solid hour of uninterrupted reading in for my English literature class, I found myself talking to my belly button.

"Now you two settle down in there so Mommy can get some reading in before Daddy gets home and we have to leave." Gordon had been invited by Chad Hanks to stand in on the blessing of his new son that weekend in Oakley. Since the midsemester stress level was high for both of us, Gordon decided to take a few days off from the grocery store so we could make a weekend of our little trip. We both needed a getaway, so the timing was actually perfect.

Curt, who was sitting at the table eating a bowl of colorful cereal for lunch, found my one-sided conversation somewhat amusing.

"Molly Mommy," he stated aloud, obviously finding humor in the mere notion that I would soon be taking on the role of a mother.

I cocked my head while my laser ray eyes attempted to bore holes into my little brother. "Something funny?"

"No. Well, yeah, a little."

"What?" I didn't want to sound defensive, but how could I help it when I was already feeling self-conscious about taking on this role. The last thing I needed was a little brother rubbing salt into my wounds of insecurity.

"I was just thinking back to when we were kids and you were such a tomboy. Maybe it was just the fact that you were older than me, but as I remember it, you could outrun, outclimb, outshoot, and out-everything me and all of my friends that came over after school. I was jealous because not only were my friends in awe of your athletic abilities, but they all had major crushes on you. That used to irritate me to no end, probably because I never saw you as a 'girl,' only as one of the guys. Now you're about to be a mom—a real diaper-changing, nose-wiping, PB&J-making mom. It's all a little surreal."

Well, what do you say to that? I had no clue, so I just shrugged and went back to my reading, only to be interrupted half a sentence later by the phone.

"Will you get that?" I asked Curt. Once I was situated on the couch, I almost needed a forklift to get me back on my feet.

Again, I tried to concentrate on my reading, but I couldn't help overhearing Curt's conversation.

"Hello. Hey, what's up? Uh-huh. Uh-huh. Oh, about three weeks ago, why?" (Pause.) "NO! No way! Really? Serious? Uh-huh. Uh-huh. Okay. Just a minute and I'll ask."

Curt lowered the phone and looked over at me with a somewhat panicked expression. "When are you leaving for Oakley?"

"As soon as Gordon gets home, and we can make it out the door."

"What? One, two hours?"

"Yeah, at the most. Why? What's going on?"

"It's Mom. My mission call came from Salt Lake. She's got it in her hands right now."

"Seriously?" I nearly screamed and then asked the obvious question "So, what does it say? Where are you going?"

"I don't know. She doesn't know yet. She wants me to come home tonight with you two and open it when Dad gets home."

That totally sounded like our mother; always wanting to turn each moment like this into a special event. And even though my patience level was screaming *"Open it right now!"*, my rational half was glad that Mom made such occasions into something memorable for the entire family.

"Sure, no problem. Tell her we'll be there by dinnertime."

Curt put the phone back up to his ear. "Did you hear that?" He asked. "Great. See ya in a few hours."

The minute Curt hung up the phone, he turned to me again.

"I gotta call Amy!"

"Yes, you do! She'd kill you if you didn't. Hey, and while you're at it, why don't you invite her to come with us. It'll help keep her mind off of the basketball tournament she's missing out on this weekend."

❊❊❊

Three hours and twenty-seven minutes later when the four of us entered the house of my childhood, the smell of something incredibly yummy overwhelmed my senses. As we approached the table, I'd even forgotten about the mission call, I was so excited to get whatever smelled so delicious into my mouth and stomach.

Dad and Dusty were seated and the lasagna was already on the table. Dusty looked a little put out having to wait for dinner. The kid had no idea how easy he had it, essentially living as an "only child."

Curt practically skidded to a halt in the kitchen. "Where is it? Where is it?"

"A quick 'hello' and introductions might be nice," said Mom as she retrieved a large white envelope from the counter and tucked it securely in her folded arms.

Curt knew our mother well enough and decided to play along, spilling out a hasty greeting. "Hey, Mom, how was your day? You remember Amy, right? Amy, Mom. Mom, Amy. Okay, can I have my letter now?"

Mom rolled her eyes and handed over the envelope.

Curt impetuously threw his arms around our mother, lifting her in the air and then kissing her on the cheek.

"Wow! Now *that* was a greeting!" said Mom.

"I just can't believe it's finally here."

Dusty's voice broke into the laughter. "So, open it already. I'm starved."

Dad shot Dusty a quick warning glance, so he slumped down into his chair and folded his arms.

Curt started to rip open the envelope with his finger, but then he stopped and handed it to Mom. "Here, you do it. I'm too nervous."

Mom, who always opened letters with a knife-like letter opener, pulled out a butter knife from the utensil drawer and finished the job.

From within the envelope, Mom pulled out a booklet and a single sheet of paper on Church letterhead. She attempted to hand it to Curt, but he put up his hands. "You read it, please."

Mom took a deep breath and started in. "Dear Elder Chambers: You are hereby called to serve as a missionary of The Church of Jesus Christ of Latter-day Saints. You are assigned to labor in the Oregon Portland Mission."

Upon hearing these words, the entire room came alive. First Curt hugged Mom, and then Amy, who seemed to be equally caught up in the joy of this family moment. When things died down, Mom finished the rest of the letter and then turned it around to point out the signature at the bottom.

"Look, it's signed by the prophet."

Mom handed the letter to Curt and he simply stared at it, still in amazement.

"So?" asked Dad as he observed my brother. "What do you think?"

After a few moments Curt responded with a beaming expression. "I'm totally excited. I couldn't have asked for a better call."

"Does anyone want to know what I think?" asked Dusty in a somewhat whining tone.

"Yes," Mom said, turning to my youngest brother. "By all means, tell us what you think."

"I think that even the good people of the state of Oregon like to eat dinner on time. I bet they'd understand if we celebrated the fact that Curt's finally leaving us, and joining them, over this presumably delicious dish of lasagna that's most likely cold by now."

Mom and Dad both looked at Dusty, exasperation etched into their tired faces. But since the rest of us started to laugh as we headed over to the table, they reluctantly joined in.

Chapter
TWENTY-SIX

With no homework or other responsibilities for the weekend, we decided to have a little fun. So, on Saturday, Curt, Amy, Gordon, and I took a short road trip up to Sun Valley to show Amy some of the sights. With the tail end of the ski season in full force, we were able to capture the true essence of the trendy resort town nestled in the Idaho mountains.

Even with my very pregnant belly and Amy's bad knee and crutches to slow us down, we managed to get in some window shopping in Ketchum as well as visit a few of the galleries to admire the works of art that were, obviously, way out of our price range. Later in the afternoon, we ate lunch at a cute little restaurant called Christina's before heading home. The day was both rejuvenating and exhausting. When we arrived back at Mom and Dad's on Saturday evening, all I wanted to do was crawl into bed. I had a feeling that sleep would come almost instantly. It did.

When I awoke Sunday morning, I was a bit stiff and maybe even a little achy, probably from the activities of the previous day. I hadn't really thought much about our little trek and the toll it might take on me physically, since I'm used to being active, but now I was wondering if maybe I'd overdone it. Why did I always to have to learn things the hard way?

Since it was fast Sunday, and everyone else in the house wasn't eating breakfast, Amy and I each had a quick bowl of cereal before we headed over to the church. The ward that Chad's mom attended met at eight–thirty, so the four of us were all rushing around in somewhat of a stupor in order to make it to the meetings on time.

Relief Society met first, so Amy and I found a seat on the front row and settled in. The lesson was on recognizing the promptings of the Holy Ghost in our lives. It looked like Amy was immersed in, and enjoying, the message being shared—a very good sign. I, on the other hand, couldn't seem to stay focused. Even though the chairs in the Relief Society room were cushioned, I was incredibly uncomfortable. Regardless of how often I shifted my weight, I couldn't seem to find a position that worked without one half of my rear end going numb or my ribs taking a beating. Oh, the ailments we women endure to bring babies into this world.

This uncomfortable scenario continued through the entire hour of Gospel Doctrine, which Brandon Mace happened to be teaching—go figure. I didn't want to just get up and leave—that would really seem awkward—so I did my best to stretch out my torso, hopefully allowing the babies a little more room to romp (because that's certainly what it felt like they were doing—romping or synchronized swimming. I couldn't be sure).

My feeble attempt to find a position of comfort was interrupted by Gordon as he whispered in my ear.

"You okay?"

Words weren't necessary to convey my thoughts as the two of us exchanged glances. Gordon knew me better than I knew myself—a phenomenon that was sometimes a little freaky but at the moment, comforting.

"Do you want me to rub your back?" he asked, once again in a whisper.

I let out a deep sigh. "Thanks, but no."

Now if we were lying in bed, this might have been a pretty good proposal. I loved a good back rub as much as the next person. but under the current circumstances, I didn't see how it would work. Slouching forward in the standard sacrament-meeting-back-scratch position simply wasn't feasible since it would require me to lean forward—a dangerous proposition altogether.

I resorted to propping my purse behind the small of my back and leaning into Gordon's shoulder. It was the most comfortable position I could find, and I only hoped it didn't come across to Brandon like I was some sort of love-crazed newlywed who couldn't stand being a half an inch away from my sweetheart. What I truly needed at the moment more than a back rub, or a comfortable husband, was a good ol' Lazy-boy recliner.

When sacrament meeting finally arrived, we made our way into the chapel for yet another hour to be spent on my rear end—a cruel fate, indeed, for my tired back side. Whomever proposed the three hour block of church meetings certainly didn't have pregnant women in mind. The hymns played quietly in the background while primary children, teenagers, and adults, alike, not-so-quietly attempted to locate family members as well as a vacant spot on a bench.

"Do you want me to run you home after the baby's blessing?" Gordon asked as we sat next to Curt and Amy on the end of one of the side pews.

"I'll be fine, I hope," I responded. "But I honestly don't think I can sit for the next hour and ten minutes." I sat up on the edge of the bench and attempted to rub my lower back. With all this sitting, it seemed to be aching more and more.

Gordon's eyes were filled with concern. "Is there anything I can do to help?"

"I'm afraid you've done enough," I said with a half smile and a wink. "I'll be fine—really. I just need to stand up and get some circulation in my legs. I'm going to go stand back in the gym near the stage. If I get tired I'll sit down on one of the side benches—at least until I can't stand it any more."

Gordon reached up and ran one of his fingers through my hair, combing it back behind my ear and then touching my dangling earring with the tip of his finger. "Do you want me to go back with you?"

"Maybe after the blessing," I suggested. "For now just stay here. You don't want to have to walk the entire length of the gym and chapel to get up there when it's time."

Gordon cocked his head to the side to get a better look at my face. His eyebrows creased as he spoke. "You sure you're okay?"

"I'll be fine."

Gordon braced my elbow as I stood up and I almost felt like an invalid. As I wobbled back to the gym that was adjoining the chapel, I ran the math in my head. *Eleven more weeks!* How would I ever make it eleven more weeks? I certainly wasn't going to get any smaller—or more comfortable.

And, what had I been thinking, taking a full load of classes this semester? Everyone was right, I *was* a lunatic! But, how was I supposed to know that I'd feel like an alien life form had taken over my entire being? I was used to always being in control of my body. I could maintain the ideal weight through diet and exercise. If I was tired, I could get more sleep. If I was hungry, I could get something to eat. But with this pregnancy, there were so many factors that were totally out of my control.

By the time I reached the side of the gym and casually propped my elbow against the stage, the bishop was at the pulpit, ready to start the meeting. Announcements were made, followed by the opening hymn and prayer. I was more than ready to take Gordon up on his offer to take me home after the blessing. As much as I wanted to hear the testimonies of old friends, my lower back was really starting to ache.

The next thing I knew, a few men were heading up to the front of the chapel. The sight of Brandon blessing Chad Hanks's baby surrounded by my own husband and the bishopric was a little surreal. Brandon, however, gave a beautiful blessing and I knew in my heart that some day he would be a great husband for some lucky lady. As I watched all of this transpire, I couldn't help but think to the future and the blessings Gordon would be able to give our children. My heart warmed at the thought.

Just as the final words of the blessing were said, a sudden warm and wet sensation began to travel down my legs leaving a small but conspicuous puddle between my feet. A gripping fear seized my heart. Had I simply wet my pants, I'd be totally embarrassed and even humiliated, but this wasn't the case.

As I stood frozen, staring at my wet shoes, I realized that someone was approaching me. When I glanced up, Gordon was standing in front of me looking from my face to my feet and then back to my face. His expression was a mixture of bafflement and amusement.

Since the sacrament hymn was playing, he leaned into my ear. "You couldn't make it to the bathroom?"

Had the situation been different, I might have either laughed at Gordon, or punched him in the arm, or both. But, I was still in a state of shock. When all I could do was stare expressionlessly into his face, he finally picked up on the fact that something might be wrong.

"You just stand here, and I'll go get some paper towels to clean this up."

He was about to walk away, when I reached out and grabbed his arm.

"We need to get to the hospital."

Gordon's face suddenly paled as realization set in. "Molly, it's not time yet. You're not ready." Gordon put his hands on my stomach. "*They're* not ready."

Actually hearing the words that I knew to be true was too much. Tears spilled from my eyes as Gordon pulled me into an embrace, his strong arms wrapped around me as well as our unborn children. The security I felt in his arms gave me a glimmer of hope that maybe all of this might turn out okay.

After only a brief moment, though, Gordon pulled me back and looked into my face.

"You're right. We *do* need to get you to the hospital."

Gordon quickly shifted into automatic pilot, taking control of the situation. After pulling the folded bulletin and a pen from his suit pocket, he scrawled a brief note and handed it to Sister Poulton who was sitting nearby, with instructions to give it to Curt as soon as the meeting ended. Then, after cleaning up the puddle with some paper towels, he led me out to our rusty old Suburban for the twenty mile trek north to Burley, and Cassia Regional Medical Center.

While I sat next to him, completely lost in my own frantic thoughts mixed with an ample dose of prayer, I was only partially aware he made a call to my parents informing them of the situation. At some point, I realized he was gently taping me on the shoulder with the cell phone.

"Do you want to talk to your mom?"

Initially, I wanted to say no because I knew that this would only end in my uncontrollable tears. But in truth, I desperately wanted to talk to my mother. I wanted her to be with me right now, even if it was only her voice through the phone.

"Hello." My voice sounded hollow, even to my own ears.

"Honey, Dad and I are going to meet you at the hospital as soon as we can get there." There was a slight pause before she continued. "Are you okay?"

I shook my head back and forth as if she could see me. The tears started afresh as I spoke. "Mom, it's too early. I'm only at twenty-nine weeks—barely into my third trimester."

Mom's voice was calming as usual. "With today's modern medicine, anything is possible. We'll just have to rely on the Lord. Okay, honey?"

I nodded but couldn't speak, so I handed the phone back to

Gordon. He said a few more things to my mom and then placed the phone on the seat between us.

The remainder of the ride to Burley was made in silence, probably because Gordon and I were both too busy praying to say much else. And what was there to say anyway? The reality of the situation was painfully obvious. I'd read enough about pregnancy and childbirth over the past six months to know that it was too early to be delivering these babies. On the other hand, once the water breaks, there aren't too many alternatives. The bag of water protects the babies from infection. Once that barrier is no longer intact, their safe environment has been compromised. Infection could easily set in.

When we arrived at the emergency room door, Gordon insisted on running in and bringing out a wheelchair for me. Even though I was feeling okay physically, I was too numb emotionally to argue.

I was amazed how quickly my treatment began. While Gordon was checking me in, a nurse wheeled me on over to labor and delivery and I was hooked up to every monitor imaginable, not to mention poked and pricked for an IV and various tests. This wasn't the standard emergency room experience I'd endured in the past for various sports injuries, and, I had to admit, I was grateful that my condition was given priority. My worry level at the moment was high enough. I didn't need any extra burdens.

After the initial flurry of nurse activity in my room finally settled down, Gordon arrived, followed shortly by the attending obstetrician on duty—a woman who looked to be about the same age as my mom. She had a kind face and a warm disposition, and I began to feel just a little bit of hope.

"Well, Mrs. Nelson. Looks like your little ones want to make an early appearance." The doctor proceeded to hold up a small cardboard wheel and rotate it around until certain numbers matched up. "You're at twenty-nine weeks."

Her words hung in the air for far too long before she continued, "It would be my recommendation that we administer a steroid as soon as possible to help with the babies' lung development. We'll also continue to monitor you and see if we can delay this delivery just a bit—hopefully another twenty-four hours. But, I guess, we'll see."

"What does all of this mean?" Gordon asked. "Are the babies going to be okay arriving so early?"

"Honestly, we just don't know at this point. But I will tell you that with technology these days, the majority of babies born at twenty-nine weeks in the United States actually survive and go on to live quite normal lives. It's generally a bit of a rough start, though."

Gordon put his arm around me in an attempt to comfort my fears. I was thankful for his strength and moral support. Even though I knew that the situation was out of our hands, just having him next to me made all the difference in my troubled heart.

Shortly after Mom and Dad arrived, I was given a priesthood blessing. Even though the situation remained critical, as the words of the blessing were spoken, a sense of peace managed to envelop my entire being and calm my soul.

The next several hours were a blur. Contractions began within that first hour at the hospital. Their progression was slow but steady, and fear of the unknown still hovered—at least if I let it. Exhaustion was setting in as the hours passed and the intensity of the contractions increased. I tried to remain focused through the breathing techniques I'd read about, but after a while, I found that if I could just maintain an even pattern of deep breathing, I was more able to deal with the increasing intensity of each contraction. Through it all, Gordon remained at my side.

At some point during the twilight hours while Gordon sat next to me, holding my hand and wiping my brow with a moist washcloth, the doctor returned to the room, and proceeded to examine the long strip of paper that was coming out of one of the machines.

After a particularly intense contraction passed, she put down the strip and turned to me and Gordon. "The babies seem to be experiencing more stress during the contractions than I'm comfortable with. Both of their heartbeats are decreasing during each contraction, so it's my recommendation that we go ahead and perform a c-section at this time."

The doctor's words, though harsh with the reality of the situation, rang true to my heart. When I looked over to Gordon for reassurance, however, his face was etched with concern.

"Will I be able to go into the operating room with my wife?" Gordon asked.

"I'm afraid, Mr. Nelson, that under the circumstances, it won't be possible. But, we'll have a nurse keep you informed every step of the operation, and the minute the babies are delivered, you can go right into the NICU."

"Will I be awake to see them?" I asked, as I clutched onto Gordon's hand as if it were the only stabilizing factor in my life at the moment.

"I think it will be best if we administer a general anesthesia. You'll be completely unconscious during the operation, but as soon as you're awake, we'll take you right in to see the babies. Unfortunately, we don't have a lot of time to discuss this. I'll give you two a moment and then I'll be back with the nurse."

Another contraction started in again—this one even stronger than the one before. If it didn't take every ounce of my concentration to get through each contraction, I just might have given in to the urge to completely fall apart. But I couldn't. Not with my babies fighting for their lives—and I had a feeling that the days ahead wouldn't be any easier.

When the contraction was over, Gordon kissed my brow, and I couldn't tell where his tears began and the perspiration on my forehead ended. He held me close as if he couldn't let me go. For some strange reason, at that moment, I felt a surge of inner strength and peace, and I wasn't even sure where it came from.

I reached up to Gordon's arm and pushed him back so I could look into his face. He attempted to wipe at his eyes, but I reached for his hand and clasped it close to my heart.

"I'm going to be okay. I really am." I reached up with my right hand to wipe a trickle of moisture traveling down Gordon's cheek. "Even though this isn't the situation we'd imagined our babies would be born into, I just have this feeling . . . No, it's more than a feeling. I *know* that their spirits are strong—very strong! I can feel their strength, Gordon. We'll just have to help their little bodies get as strong as their spirits, okay?"

Gordon didn't say anything, just nodded and then kissed my cheek.

The pressure of another contraction began and my focus turned inward. I was nearly oblivious as several nurses and the doctor reentered the room. Everything happened so fast as the preparations for surgery began. I wasn't even sure when Gordon left my side during the whirlwind of events. Someone, I wasn't sure who, asked me to start counting backward from ten to one. As I looked up, I realized that I was traveling down a hallway. Even though everything around me felt rushed, like the lights flashing by on the ceiling, my heart felt at peace. Ready or not, I was about to become a mother.

"Ten, nine, eight . . ."

Chapter
TWENTY-SEVEN

"Molly. Molly, can you hear me? It's time to wake up."

I was so tired. I just wanted to sleep. Why did Mom always try to wake me up? I swear, the woman's never been tired a day in her life.

"Molly, are you awake? Do you know where you are?"

It took a great effort to finally make my mouth work. "I'm tired, just wanna sleep a little more."

"Don't you want to see your babies?"

Babies?

I wanted my eyes to open faster than they would. Did she say babies? *My* babies? I slowly reached for my stomach and though it wasn't flat, it wasn't firm and round either. It was, however, very tender to the slightest touch or movement.

I attempted to sit but immediately gave up on that idea the minute my stomach—both inside and out—let me know that it wasn't ready to cooperate. A wave of nausea overwhelmed me, and the only redeeming aspect of the entire purging experience was that my mommy was there to take care of me.

When I finally finished throwing up and wondered if there was still anything left in the world to live for, I heard that magic word again. This time from an unfamiliar voice—probably the nurse.

"General anesthesia often brings on nausea, but as soon as you're feeling better, we can wheel you in to see the babies."

"How are they—my babies?"

"They're fighters, just like you," my mom said. "And don't worry, the only time Gordon has left their side is to check on you. The poor guy—he's exhausted but refuses to get any sleep until you're awake and okay. As a matter of fact, I'd better go get him. I promised I would the minute you began to stir."

I wasn't sure how much time passed because I fell back asleep. But this time I was waking up to kisses on my forehead.

"Good morning, beautiful."

I'd heard these words many times over during the past year from this familiar voice, but never before had they made me cry—partly because I knew that at the moment I looked about as far from beautiful as was humanly possible, and partly because it was just so comforting to hear Gordon's voice and feel his gentle kiss. Had I even told him, lately, how wonderful he was and how much I truly loved him?

Again, I was struggling to open my eyes as I spoke. "Are the babies okay?"

Gordon took hold of my hand, careful not to disturb the IV, and kissed my knuckle. "Well, they're very small, and hooked up to quite a bit of stuff, but they're stable. Under the circumstances, they seem to be doing well."

Just hearing that last phrase somehow allowed me to take a deep breath. With this knowledge, I was even tempted to drift back into the land of peaceful slumber when I realized Gordon was wiping tears from the outside corners of my eyes as the moisture slipped back into my hairline.

It wasn't until that moment that I realized I didn't even know for sure the gender of my babies. "So, what are they?"

"They're beautiful, just like their mother."

I turned to Gordon and rolled my eyes, which was way too easy to do considering my nearly delirious condition.

"Oh," Gordon feigned sudden understanding. "You mean boys or girls?"

I squeezed Gordon's hand as hard as I could—which wasn't very hard at all. "You know what I mean."

Gordon chuckled. "Well, I don't think I should tell you. I think you should just come and meet them for yourself."

The heart was definitely willing but, honestly, I wasn't quite sure my head was clear enough, or my body strong enough, to make it down to the NICU. But, as usual, the heart prevailed. With some help from Gordon, the nurse, and some pretty strong pain medication, I was able to get into a wheelchair. The rest was up to Gordon—my chauffeur.

Gordon carefully pushed my wheelchair while I tried to navigate the pole connected to my IV drip with my right hand and apply pressure to a pillow placed over my stomach with my left. Could things possibly get more complicated? We looked a little peculiar, and it was quite a feat, but we were getting to where we needed to be—next to our babies.

Gordon and I actually made a pretty good pair whether we were ballroom dancing around the halls of BYU-Idaho or maneuvering a wheelchair down the halls of Cassia Regional Medical Center. If it took teamwork, we could manage. I had a feeling that the next several months, even years, were going to require an ample amount of teamwork. I also knew we'd be up to the challenge. Together, we could do anything.

When we reached the door to the NICU, Gordon pulled the wheelchair to a stop at the side of the hall, came around in front of me, and then knelt down on one knee so we were at the same eye level.

"I just wanted to remind you that they're very small—two pounds ten ounces, and two pounds fifteen ounces. They're hooked up to a lot of stuff—an IV, a ventilator, a heart monitor, an oxygen monitor, a feeding tube . . ."

I held up my hand, "I don't care. I just want to see my babies."

Gordon reached out for my hand and gently held it in both of his. "I know. I guess I just wanted to warn you so you wouldn't be too shocked."

"I'll be okay." I said these words because I desperately wanted them to be true. In reality, though, I was quite nervous and afraid of the unknown.

We entered the NICU. Several isolettes were situated in stations around the entire room and I immediately wondered which ones contained my babies. My whole body, though weary, literally ached to be near them. We had been together for so many months that it felt unnatural to be apart. It was frustrating to be confined to a wheelchair as I anxiously waited for Gordon to wheel me forward, but he stopped at a large stainless steel sink.

"We have to scrub down first."

I raised my hands and looked at the IV wondering how this would be possible, but with the assistance of a nurse, we did our best.

As we approached the corner of the NICU, Gordon pointed. "They put them together about an hour ago. The nurse said that preemie twins often do better if they're together."

Just hearing this made my heart swell with gratitude. It was comforting to know that at this difficult time, while I had been away from my babies, they still had each other—someone familiar in this new and crazy world.

When we reached the corner of the room and I looked through the glass cover at my two beautiful babies, I was overcome with emotion. It was truly amazing that through our love, Gordon and I were able to create these two beautiful and perfect babies. What had I done in this life to deserve such a miraculous blessing? Sure, they still had some growing and developing to do, but I planned to be there for these babies—always.

Gordon leaned down toward the wheelchair and placed his cheek next to mine. I'd heard people say that in a marriage 'two become one,' but the statement had never felt so literal as at that very moment when we sat together looking at our newborn babies. We were a family—an eternal union.

Gordon had been right in his description of the situation; there were numerous wires and tubes connected to almost every part of their little bodies. Maybe it seemed worse because each baby was only a little over a foot long—fourteen inches to be exact. I couldn't be sure about the color of their hair because they were each wearing a little cap—one blue, and the other pink.

Gordon, ever the gracious host, began the introductions, first reaching through the hole in the isolette to stroke the arm of the closest twin, whose back was toward us.

"Mommy, I'd like to introduce you to our son, Baby Boy Nelson. If you go around to the other side you can see that he actually has my mouth and chin—and muscles, of course."

I giggled and sniffled at the same time, and tried to blink the moisture out of my eyes since I couldn't wipe them away with my recently scrubbed hands.

Tentatively, I reached my hand in the other hole near the bottom of the isolette and touched my son's foot—the one that wasn't connected to wires. His perfect and tiny little toes were all accounted for and curled to my touch.

Then, reaching across our son, Gordon softly touched the bare shoulder of the other baby. "And this is our daughter, little miss Baby Girl Nelson—isn't she pretty?"

"Yes, she is. Very pretty." Both babies were facing each other, and it almost looked like they were holding hands the way their arms interlocked with one another.

Extending my arm farther into the isolette, I ran my hand along my daughter's leg, in total awe of its warmth and softness.

"Hello, Sweet Pea," I said in a soft voice to my daughter as I continued to stroke her leg.

"Sweet Pea?" Gordon asked with a raised eyebrow.

"It's the best I can do right now. It's a miracle I'm even speaking in complete sentences at the moment."

Gordon chose to ignore my last comment. "Maybe we should call her Sariah? Or maybe Ruth or Eliza?"

I looked over at my daughter with a smile. "Nah, I think she looks like a Breanne—or even a Katie or Katelyn."

"But what do these names mean? How are they significant?"

"What does it matter? She'll create her own meaning each day of her life. As long as she understands her potential and knows how much we love her, she'll do fine, regardless of whether her name is found in the scriptures or somewhere in church history."

Gordon was relentless. "How about an ancestor's name—like your grandma?"

I tried not to smile as I replied, "You want to name our daughter Phyllis?"

Gordon shrugged but wouldn't admit defeat.

I reached through the isolette and took hold of Gordon's hand. "You know, there's one thing I've learned through the years, and that is that it doesn't matter what people call you. You can be called Molly Mormon, or Gordon the Goofball, or Alexander the Great. In the end what does it really mean?"

Gordon looked at me with a raised eyebrow, "People call me Gordon the Goofball?"

I ignored my husband's comment since to my knowledge, *I* was the only person that ever referred to him as Gordon the Goofball, and that was a long time ago. I continued on. "The thing that matters most in this life is how you feel about yourself and what you make of yourself, not what people label you. And as far as having a family name, our children will always be Nelsons."

This brought a smile to Gordon's face. "You've got a point there."

As we continued to gaze down at our sleeping children, a thought came to me. "I know, let's make a deal. I'll name our daughter, and you can name our son as long as we personally know someone else under the age of twenty-five with the same name." I knew I was being tricky here, but this would most likely eliminate the possibility of having to someday explain to my son why he's the only Ezra, or Moses, or Mahonri Moriancumer in his entire school.

Gordon didn't say anything for quite a while as we continued to stroke the soft skin of our beautiful but tiny children. Finally, he spoke. "Okay, it's a deal."

We shook hands on the inside of the isolette, sealed by a brief kiss. When we looked back down at the babies, our daughter began to stir. The moment she opened her eyes, my heart melted.

"Oh, look, Gordon, she's awake."

"Well, hello, beautiful." This made me smile. Gordon sure knows how to charm the females in his life.

"When can I hold them?" I asked.

"I'm not sure, but the nurse told me this morning that if every-thing goes well, we will probably be able to bring them home in two months."

My heart sank. Did he say *two months?* He might as well have said *two years!*

Chapter
T W E N T Y - E I G H T

Two months and two years later . . .

"Curt, get that purple crayon out of your nose this instant!"

As I glanced to the back seat of the Suburban and looked into those startled blue eyes, I regretted using such a sharp tone. He really was a sweetheart when he wasn't getting into mischief.

Curt removed the crayon and held it out for me.

"Here, Mommy."

I reached back and took the offending crayon from my son's small hands, careful to avoid one particular end.

"Thank you, sweetie."

A few moments passed in silence while I enjoyed the passing view of the Idaho countryside. Large mechanical watering pivots were running full force in an attempt to turn the brown fields green. I loved living in Idaho and it looked like we'd be staying. Gordon had just graduated from ISU with a master's degree in Nuclear Engineering and had secured a position at the INEEL (Idaho National Engineering and Environmental Laboratory).

"Mommy," Curt's little voice broke into my reverie. "I wanna cookie."

Gordon tilted his head back and replied on my behalf. "Not right now, son." Then, turning to face me, he commented, "He's just like his Uncle Curt, appetite and all."

"You think he gets his appetite from my brother?" I said with a chuckle. "I was thinking little Curt takes after his daddy."

Gordon arched back in the driver's seat and patted his perfectly flat stomach. "I can't help it if I like your gourmet cooking."

"It's hardly gourmet, but it's improved quite a bit over the last couple of years."

"Yeah, your brother will be impressed."

I held up my hands. "Hey, now, don't get any brilliant ideas. Just because he's moving back to Pocatello in the fall doesn't mean I want him living with us again. I can only handle one Curt at a time and I think I'll keep this little guy, thank you very much!" I pointed my thumb to the back seat, and shot a glance at my son who was now attempting to bite the head off of a little plastic Winnie the Pooh figurine.

After retrieving a graham cracker from the diaper bag, I handed it to my son and plucked poor, slobbery, Pooh Bear from his clutches. I swear, people probably think we never feed the kid!

"What time is it?" I asked. "Mom will kill us if we're late."

Gordon raised his wrist to examine his watch. "We're doing fine. Curt's flight doesn't come in until 12:06. It's only 11:30.

I took a deep breath and tried to relax, but I was excited to see my little brother after two whole years. "How much do you think he's changed?" I asked.

"Probably a lot," said Gordon. "Missions have a way of doing that. But the change is always for the better. I know it's a cliché, but they really are 'the best two years'—at least as far as spiritual growth goes."

"Well, Curt's not the only one who's changed," I said. "Before he left, Amy seemed to be warming up to the gospel. I even thought she'd finish taking the discussions. But while he's been gone, she's gradually headed in the opposite direction."

"Have the two stayed in touch this whole time?" asked Gordon.

"I'm pretty sure they have. It'll be interesting to see what happens in the fall when she's back from Tulsa and the semester starts."

"You just never know. Life can be full of surprises."

"That's for sure," I replied.

Fifteen minutes later we pulled into the parking lot of the Magic Valley Regional Airport in Twin Falls. My entire family would be there for Curt's arrival—Mom, Dad, and our youngest brother, Dusty (who would be leaving on his own mission within the coming year), Alex, Tiffany, and their three little ones, Blake, and his new bride, Josi, and, of course, the Nelson family.

Just as Gordon turned off the ignition, a small whimper came from the back seat. I quickly got out of our mammoth sized vehicle and opened the back door.

"Well, look who finally woke up," I said as I unfastened the safety straps and removed Caitlyn from her car seat. She'd slept the entire trip from Pocatello—definitely the more mellow of the Nelson twins.

Gordon removed the double stroller—my lifeline to sanity in the outside world—from the back of the Suburban and placed Curt in front while I placed Caitlyn in the back. Slowly, we headed across the large parking lot enjoying the warmth of the spring day.

I turned to Gordon as we made our way toward the terminal in the distance. "Curt's not going to even recognize these two. They'd barely made it home from the hospital when he left."

"Well, he may not recognize them," said Gordon, "but you're looking pretty much the same as you did when he lived with us."

I glanced down and patted the bulge in my increasingly expanding stomach. "Yeah, I guess you're right. But this time, there's only one in there to kick my ribs and give me heartburn in the middle of the night."

"Yeah," Gordon replied, "but look at what you got in return."

As I attempted to analyze Gordon's remark, I looked down in the stroller at the two strawberry blond babies who initiated me into motherhood. My little Curt and Caitlyn had literally turned every day of the past two years of my life upside-down and inside-out. And yet, everything about them made my life right—complete.

During their two-month stay at the hospital after their premature birth, I thought my heart would never mend as I helplessly watched them endure test after test and treatment after treatment. But each day, the twins grew stronger, and each day my heart grew larger and fuller.

Before their birth, I honestly had no idea of the true capability of my heart to unconditionally love another human being—let alone two. Motherhood does amazing things.

Now, with thriving two-year-olds to keep life interesting, and another new baby on the way, our family had taken on a comfortable routine. Unlike a few years ago, I was actually quite confident in my role as mother—confident and happy.

Oh, I was still far from perfect. And I definitely had moments when I wondered if maybe it might be a little more fun to have fewer responsibilities and more time to shoot hoops. But all it took was a bright-eyed look from Caitlyn or a spontaneous hug from Curt, and I knew without a doubt that I had the best and most important gig in the entire universe.

I was a Mommy!

About the Author

Tamra Norton is a full-time keeper of the peace, feeder of things that growl, and supreme commander of all things coming and going from her home in Spring, Texas.

She attended Ricks College and Idaho State University, where she majored in English. She began her writing career with a column published in the *Fort Bend Sun*. Called "The Home Front," it depicted the antics of home life. Her passion, however, is writing fiction.

Tamra enjoys reading in the bathtub, camping in the living room, and dancing in the kitchen. When she isn't gazing vacantly into the computer screen in the middle of the night, she is home schooling her children and avoiding the guilt associated with lack of exercise and overindulgence of chocolate.

Tamra is the proud missionary mom of a son serving in the Oregon Portland Mission. She and her husband, Dennis, a research and development engineer in the Houston oil industry, have seven children.

Tamra welcomes comments from her readers. Feel free to visit her website at www.tamranorton.com, or send her an e-mail at tamra@tamranorton.com.

0 26575 78316 2